Nightmares
of Eminent Persons

AND OTHER STORIES BY

BERTRAND RUSSELL

ILLUSTRATED BY
CHARLES W. STEWART

Simon and Schuster · New York · 1955

LIBRARY OF CONGRESS CATALOG CARD NUMBER: 54-12360
MANUFACTURED IN THE UNITED STATES OF AMERICA
BY KINGSPORT PRESS, INC., KINGSPORT, TENN.

PREFACE

It is only fair to warn the reader that not all the stories in this volume are intended to cause amusement. Of the "Nightmares," some are purely fantastic, while others represent possible, though not probable, horrors. "Zahatopolk" is designed to be completely serious. The last story, "Faith and Mountains," may strike some readers as fantastic, but, if so, they must have led sheltered lives, as appears from the following:

"Taking its cue from the Coronation of Queen Elizabeth II of England this year, the National Pickle Association started a search for an American girl with the name of Elizabeth Pickle to be the ruler of Pickledom during 1953. The Peanut Journal and Nut World." (Quoted from the Observer, *June 28, 1953.)*

I wish Elizabeth Pickle all success!

CONTENTS

INTRODUCTION

The following "Nightmares" might be called "Signposts to Sanity." Every isolated passion is, in isolation, insane; sanity may be defined as a synthesis of insanities. Every dominant passion generates a dominant fear, the fear of its non-fulfillment. Every dominant fear generates a nightmare, sometimes in the form of an explicit and conscious fanaticism, sometimes in a paralyzing timidity, sometimes in an unconscious or subconscious terror which finds expression only in dreams. The man who wishes to preserve sanity in a dangerous world should summon in his own mind a parliament of fears, in which each in turn is voted absurd by all the others. The dreamers of the following nightmares did not adopt this technique; it is hoped that the reader will have more wisdom.

Nightmares
of Eminent Persons

The Queen of Sheba's Nightmare

PUT NOT THY TRUST IN PRINCES

The Queen of Sheba, returning from her visit to King Solomon, was riding through the desert on a white ass with her Grand Vizier beside her on an ass of more ordinary color. As they rode, she discoursed reminiscently about the wealth and wisdom of Solomon.

"I had always thought," she said, "that I do pretty well in the way of royal splendor, and I had hoped beforehand that I should be able to hold my own, but when I had seen his possessions I had no spirit left in me. But the treasures of his palace are as nothing to the treasures of his mind. Ah, my dear Vizier, what wisdom, what knowledge of life, what sagacity his conversation displays! If you had as much political sagacity in your whole body as that king has in his little finger, we should have none of these troubles in my kingdom. But it is not only in wealth and wisdom that he is matchless. He is also (though perhaps I am the only one privileged to know this) a supreme poet. He gave me as we parted a jeweled volume in his own inimitable handwriting, telling in language of exquisite beauty the joy that he had experienced in my company. There are passages celebrating some of my more intimate charms which I should blush to show you; but there are portions of this book which I may perhaps read to you to beguile the evenings of our journey through the desert. In this exquisite volume not only are his own words such as any lady would love to hear from amorous lips, but by a quintessence of imaginative sympathy he has attributed to me poetic words which I should be glad to have uttered. Never again, I am convinced, shall I find such perfect union, such entire harmony, and such penetration into the recesses of the soul. My public duties, alas, compel me to return to my kingdom, but I shall carry with me to my dying day the knowledge that there is on earth one man worthy of my love."

"Your Majesty," replied the Vizier, "it is not for me to instill doubts into the royal breast, but to all those who serve you, it is incredible that among men your equal should exist."

At this moment, emerging out of the sunset, a weary figure appeared on foot.

"Who may this be?" said the Queen.

"Some beggar, your Majesty," said the Grand Vizier. "I strongly advise you to steer clear of him."

But a certain dignity in the aspect of the approaching stranger seemed to her indicative of something more than a beggar. And in spite of the Grand Vizier's protests she turned her ass toward him. "And who may you be?" she said.

His answer dispelled at once the Grand Vizier's suspicions,

for he spoke in the most polished idiom of the court of Sheba: "Your Majesty," he said, "my name is Beelzebub, but it is probably unknown to you, as I seldom travel far from the land of Canaan. Who you are, I know. And not only who you are, but whence you come, and what fancies inspire your sunset meditations. You have come, I know, from visiting that wise king who, though my humble guise might seem to belie my words, has been for many years my firm friend. I am convinced that he has told you concerning himself all that he wishes you to know. But if—though the hypothesis seems rash —there is anything that you wish to know concerning him beyond what he has seen fit to tell, you have but to ask me, for he has no secrets from me."

"You surprise me," said the Queen, "but I see that our conversation will be too long to be conducted conveniently while you walk and I ride. My Grand Vizier shall dismount and give his ass to you."

With an ill grace the Grand Vizier complied.

"I suppose," the Queen said, "that your conversations with Solomon were mainly concerned with statecraft and matters of deep wisdom. I, as a queen not unrenowned for wisdom, also conversed with him on these topics; but some of our conversation—so at least I flatter myself—revealed a side of him less intimately known, I should imagine, to you than to me. And some of the best of this he put into a book which he gave to me as we parted. This book contains many beauties, for example, a lovely description of the spring."

"Ah," said Beelzebub, "and does he in this description speak of the voice of the turtle?"

"Why, yes," said the Queen. "But how did you guess?"

"Oh, well," Beelzebub replied, "he was proud of having

5

noticed the turtle talking in the spring and liked to bring it in when he could."

"Some of his compliments," the Queen resumed, "particularly pleased me. I had practiced Hebrew during the journey to Jerusalem, but was not sure whether I had mastered it adequately. I was therefore delighted when he said, 'Thy speech is comely.'"

"Very nice of him," said Beelzebub. "And did he at the same time remark that your Majesty's temples are like a piece of pomegranate?"

"Well, really," said the Queen, "this is getting uncanny! He did say so, and I thought it rather an odd remark. But how on earth did you guess?"

"Well," Beelzebub replied, "you know all great men have kinks, and one of his is a peculiar interest in pomegranates."

"It is true," said the Queen, "that some of his comparisons are a little odd. He said, for instance, that my eyes were like the fish pools of Heshbon."

"I have known him," said Beelzebub, "to make even stranger comparisons. Did he ever compare your Majesty's nose to the Tower of Lebanon?"

"Good gracious," said the Queen, "this is too much! He did make that comparison. But you are persuading me that you must have some more intimate source of knowledge than I had suspected."

"Your Majesty," Beelzebub replied, "I fear that what I have to say may cause you some pain. The fact is that some of his wives were friends of mine, and through them I got to know him well."

"Yes, but how about this love poem?"

"Well, you see, when he was young, while his father was

still alive, he had to take more trouble. In those days he loved a farmer's virtuous daughter, and only overcame her scruples by his poetic gifts. Afterwards, he thought it a pity the gifts should be wasted, and he gave a copy to each of his ladies in turn. You see, he was essentially a collector, as you must have noticed when you went over his house. By long practice, he made each in turn think herself supreme in his affections; and you, dear lady, are his last and most signal triumph."

"Oh, the wretch!" she said. "Never again will I be deceived by the perfidy of man. Never again will I let flattery blind me. To think that I, who throughout my dominions am accounted the wisest of women, should have permitted myself to be so misled!"

"Nay, dear lady," said Beelzebub, "be not so cast down, for Solomon is not only the wisest man in his dominions, but the wisest of all men, and will be known as such through countless ages. To have been deceived by him is scarcely matter for shame."

"Perhaps you are right," she said, "but it will take time to heal the wound to my pride."

"Ah, sweet Queen," Beelzebub replied, "how happy could I be if I could hasten the healing work of Time! Far be it from me to imitate the wiles of that perfidious monarch. From me shall flow only simple words dictated by the spontaneous sentiments of the heart. To you, the Peerless, the Incomparable, the Matchless Jewel of the South, I would give—if you permit it—whatever balm a true appreciation of your worth can offer."

"Your words are soothing," she replied, "but can you match his splendors? Have you a palace that can compare with his? Have you such store of precious stones? Such robes, purveying the aroma of myrrh and frankincense? And, more important than any of these, have you a wisdom equal to his?"

"Lovely Sheba," he replied, "I can satisfy you on every point. I have a palace far grander than Solomon's. I have a far greater store of precious stones. My robes of state are as numerous as the stars in the sky. And as for wisdom, his is not a match for mine. Solomon is surprised that, although the rivers flow into the sea, yet the sea is not full. I know why this is, and will explain it to your Majesty on some long winter evening. To come to a more serious lapse, it was after he had seen you that he said 'there is no new thing under the sun.' Can you doubt that in his thoughts he was comparing you unfavorably with the farmer's daughter of his youth? And can any man be accounted wise who, having beheld you, does not at once perceive that here is a new wonder of beauty and majesty? No! In a competition of wisdom I have nothing to fear from him."

With a smile, half of resignation concerning the past, and half of dawning hope for a happier future, she turned her eyes upon Beelzebub and said: "Your words are beguiling. I made a long journey from my kingdom to Solomon's, and I thought I had seen what is most noteworthy on this earth. But, if you speak truth, your kingdom, your palace, and your wisdom, all surpass Solomon's. May I extend my journey by a visit to your dominion?"

He returned her smile with one in which the appearance of love barely concealed the reality of triumph. "I can imagine no greater delight," he said, "than that you should allow me this opportunity to place my poor riches at your feet. Let us go while yet the night is young. But the way is dark and difficult, and infested by fierce robbers. If you are to be safe, you must trust yourself completely to my guidance."

"I will," she said. "You have given me new hope."

At this moment they arrived at a measureless cavern in the mountainside. Holding aloft a flaming torch, Beelzebub led the way through long tunnels and tortuous passages. At last they emerged into a vast hall lit by innumerable lamps. The walls and roof glittered with precious stones whose scintillating facets flashed back the light of the lamps. In solemn state, three hundred silver thrones were ranged round the walls.

"This is indeed magnificent," said the Queen.

"Oh," said Beelzebub, "this is only my second-rate hall of audience. You shall now see the Presence Chamber."

Opening a hitherto invisible door, he led her into another hall, more than twice as large as the first, more than twice as brilliantly lit, and more than twice as richly jeweled. Round three walls of this hall were seven hundred golden thrones. On the fourth wall were two thrones, composed entirely of precious stones, diamonds, sapphires, rubies, huge pearls, bound together by some strange art which the Queen could not fathom.

"This," he said, "is my great hall, and of the two jeweled thrones, one is mine and the other shall be yours."

"But who," she said, "is to occupy the seven hundred golden thrones?"

"Ah well," he said, "you will know that in due course."

As he spoke, a queenly figure, only slightly less splendid than the Queen of Sheba, glided in and occupied the first of the golden thrones. With something of a shock, the Queen of Sheba recognized Solomon's chief consort.

"I had not expected to meet her here," she said with a slight tremor.

"Ah well," said Beelzebub, "you see I have magic powers. And while I have been wooing you, I have been telling this good lady also that Solomon is not all he seems. She listened to my words as you have listened, and she has come."

Scarcely had he finished speaking when another lady, whom also the Queen of Sheba recognized from her visit to Solomon's harem, entered and occupied the second golden throne. Then came a third, a fourth, a fifth, until it seemed as if the procession would never end. At last all the seven hundred golden thrones were occupied.

"You may be wondering," Beelzebub remarked in silken tones, "about the three hundred silver thrones. All these are by now occupied by Solomon's three hundred concubines. All the thousand in this hall and the other have heard from me words not unlike those that you have heard, all have been convinced by me, and all are here."

"Perfidious monster!" exclaimed the Queen. "How could I have had the simplicity to let myself be deceived a second time! Henceforth I will reign alone, and no male shall ever again be given a chance to deceive me. Good-by, foul fiend! If you ever venture into my dominions, you shall suffer the fate that your villainy has deserved."

"No, good lady," Beelzebub replied, "I am afraid you do not quite realize the position. I showed you the way in, but only I can find the way out. This is the abode of the dead, and you are here for all eternity—but not for all eternity on the diamond throne beside mine. That you will occupy only until you are superseded by an even more divine queen, the last Queen of Egypt."

These words produced in her such a tumult of rage and despair that she awoke.

"I fear," said the Grand Vizier, "that your Majesty has had troubled dreams."

Mr. Bowdler's Nightmare

FAMILY BLISS

Mr. Bowdler, the highly meritorious author of *The Family Shakespeare*, which the most innocent young lady could read without a blush, never showed in waking life any doubt of the usefulness of his labors. It would seem, however, that somewhere within the depths of that good man's unconscious there must have lurked a still small voice, malign and mocking. It was his practice on Sundays to dispense liberal helpings of pork to his family and not least to himself. It was accompanied by boiled potatoes and cabbage, and followed by roly-poly pudding. For himself, though not for the rest of the household, there was a moderate portion of ale. After this repast, it was his custom to take a brisk walk. But once, when snow and sleet were falling heavily, he permitted himself to break through his usual routine and rest in a chair with a good book. The good book, however, was not very interesting, and he fell alseep. In his sleep he was afflicted by the following nightmare:

* * *

Mr. Bowdler was believed by all the world, and is still believed by many, to have been a pattern of all the virtues. He had, however, at one time dreadful reason to doubt whether, in fact, he was all that his neighbors believed him.

In his youth he wrote a scathing attack upon Wilkes (of Wilkes & Liberty), whom he considered, not wholly without reason, to be a libertine. Wilkes was, by this time, past his prime, and no longer capable of taking such vengeance as in earlier years would have been natural to him. He left in his will a considerable sum of money to young Mr. Spiffkins, with the sole condition that Mr. Spiffkins, to the best of his ability, should bring disaster upon the head of Mr. Bowdler. Mr. Spiffkins, I regret to say, unhesitatingly accepted the unscrupulous legacy.

With a view to carrying out the provisions of Wilkes's will, he visited Mr. Bowdler under the guise of seeming friendship. He found Mr. Bowdler in the fullest enjoyment of perfect family bliss. He had a child on each knee, and was saying: "Ride a cock horse to Banbury Cross." Presently two other children began to clamor: "Our turn now, Papa!" and they, in their turn, were provided with oscillatory ecstasy. Mrs. Bowdler, buxom, good-natured, and smiling, surveyed the happy scene while she bustled about preparing the tea.

Mr. Spiffkins, with that exquisite tact which had caused Mr. Wilkes to select him, led the conversation to those literary topics which he knew to be dear to the heart of Mr. Bowdler, and to the principles which had guided that gentleman in making the works of great men not unfit to be put into the hands of little women. The utmost harmony prevailed until at last, after tea was over, and Mrs. Bowdler could be seen through the open door of the pantry washing up the teacups, Mr. Spiffkins rose to go. As he was saying good-by, he remarked:

"I am impressed, dear Mr. Bowdler, by your quiverful of domestic blessings, but having carefully studied all the omissions that you have made in the works of the Bard of Avon, I am compelled to conclude that these smiling infants owe their existence to parthenogenesis."

Mr. Bowdler, red with fury, shouted: "Get out!" and slammed the door in the face of Mr. Spiffkins. But alas, Mrs. Bowdler, in spite of the clatter of the teacups, had overheard the dreadful word. What it meant she could not imagine, but since she did not know it, and her husband disapproved of it, she had no doubt that it must be a bad word.

It was not the sort of matter about which she could ask her husband. He would only have replied: "My dear, it means something about which good women do not think." She was therefore left to her own devices. She knew, of course, all about Genesis, but the first half of the word remained obscure to her. One day, greatly daring, she stole into her husband's library while he was out and, fetching down the Classical Dictionary, read all that it had to say about the Parthenon. But still the meaning of this strange word eluded her. There was nothing about the Parthenon in Genesis, and nothing about Genesis in the frieze of the Parthenon.

The more her researches were baffled, the more the subject obsessed her. Her housework, which had been impeccable, became slovenly. She brooded. And one Wednesday she even forgot to provide shrimps for tea, a thing which she had not forgotten on any Wednesday since the happy day when she was united to Mr. Bowdler in the holy bonds of wedlock.

At last matters reached a point at which Mr. Bowdler felt it necessary to summon medical assistance. The doctor asked innumerable questions, tapped Mrs. Bowdler's forehead with a little wooden mallet, felt her bumps, and finally bled her, but all to no avail. At last he said:

"Well, my dear lady, I fear there is only one cure for your complaint, and that is *edax rerum* (his pedantic name for time). We must look to time, the great healer."

"Pray, dear Doctor, where is *edax rerum* to be obtained?" said Mrs. Bowdler.

"Anywhere," the doctor replied.

Although she had not much faith in his wisdom, for, after all, she had not disclosed to him the source of the trouble, she nevertheless went to the family apothecary and asked him whether he would supply her with *edax rerum*. He blushed and stammered and said: "Madam, that is not the sort of thing that nice ladies ought to want."

She retired in confusion.

Baffled in one direction, her desperate state impelled her to an attempt in another. It was part of her husband's duty to read books of the sort that he wished to suppress, and by examining the bills of booksellers on his desk, she came to know the name and address of one whom, judging by the items supplied to Mr. Bowdler, she thought likely to possess literature even on so dreadful a subject as that in which she was interested. Thickly veiled, she ventured into his premises, and boldly said:

"Sir, I desire a book to instruct me on parthenogenesis."

"Madam," he replied, observing such charms of person as her veil did not conceal, "parthenogenesis is what you will not learn about if you come upstairs with me."

Horrified and frightened, she fled.

Only one hope remained to her, a hope involving a desperate resolve and a courage of which she almost doubted herself to be possessed. She remembered that her husband, in order to complete his *Family Shakespeare*, that boon to every decent household, had been forced, painful as the task undoubtedly must have been, to read the unexpurgated works of that regrettably free-spoken author. She knew that he possessed, behind the locked doors of a certain bookcase, a pre-Bowdlerian Shakespeare, in which all the passages that he had wisely seen fit to omit were underlined in order to facilitate the work of the printer. "Surely," she thought, "where so much has been omitted, I am sure to find the word 'parthenogenesis' in some underlined passage, and I cannot doubt that the context will show me the meaning of this word."

One day, when her husband had been invited to address a congress of virtuous booksellers, she crept into his study, found the key to the locked bookcase after some search in his desk, unlocked the fatal doors, and extracted the tattered volume with its appalling lore. Page after page she perused, but nowhere did she find the word she sought. She found, however, many things that she had not sought. Horrified, yet fascinated, repelled, and yet absorbed, she read on and on, oblivious of the passage of time. Suddenly she became aware that the door was open and that her husband stood in the doorway. In tones of horror, he exclaimed:

"Good God, Maria, what volume do I behold in your

hands? Are you not aware that poison drips from its pages, that the infection of lewd thoughts leaps from its every letter into the unguarded female mind? Have you forgotten that it has been my life's task to preserve the innocent from such pollution? Oh, that failure so dire should come upon me in the very bosom of my own family!"

With that, the good man burst into tears, tears of mortification and sorrow, aye, and of righteous anger too. Suddenly aware of her sin, she dropped the volume, fled to her chamber, and burst into heart-rending sobs.

But penitence was of no avail. She had read too much. Not one word of what she had read could she forget. Round and round in her head went shameful words and dreadful images of horrid joys. Hour by hour and day by day, the obsession grew more complete, until at last she was seized with an ungovernable frenzy, and had to be taken to the asylum, shouting Shakespearian obscenities to the whole street as she was borne away. Mr. Bowdler, when her terrible words were no longer audible, fell upon his knees, asking his Maker for what sin he was thus punished. Unlike you and me, he was unable to find the answer.

The Psychoanalyst's Nightmare

It is the fate of rebels to found new orthodoxies. How this is happening to psychoanalysis has been persuasively set forth in Dr. Robert Lindner's *Prescription for Rebellion*. Many psychoanalysts, one must suppose, have their secret misgivings. It was one of these who, though orthodox in his waking hours, was afflicted during sleep by the following deeply disquieting nightmare:

* * *

In the hall of the Limbo Rotary Club, presided over by a statue of Shakespeare, the Committee of Six was holding its annual meeting. The Committee consisted of: Hamlet, Lear, Macbeth, Othello, Antony, and Romeo. All these six, while they yet lived on earth, had been psychoanalyzed by Mac-

17

beth's doctor, Dr. Bombasticus. Macbeth, before the doctor had taught him to speak ordinary English, had asked, in the stilted language that in those days he employed, "Canst thou not minister to a mind diseas'd?" "Why, yes," replied the doctor, "of course I can. It is only necessary that you should lie on my sofa and talk, and I will undertake to listen at a guinea a minute." Macbeth at once agreed. And the other five agreed at various times.

Macbeth told how at one time he had fancies of homicide, and in a long dream saw all that Shakespeare relates. Fortunately, he met the doctor in time, who explained that he saw Duncan as a father figure, and Lady Macbeth as a mother. The doctor, with some difficulty, persuaded him that Duncan was not really his father, so he became a loyal subject. Malcolm and Donalbain died young, and Macbeth succeeded in due course. He remained devoted to Lady Macbeth, and together they spent their days in good works. He encouraged boy scouts, and she opened bazaars. He lived to a great age, respected by all except the porter.

The statue, which had a gramophone in its interior, remarked at this stage: "All our yesterdays have lighted fools the way to dusty death."

Macbeth started, and said, "Damn that statue. That fellow Shakespeare wrote a most libelous work about me. He only knew me when I was young, before I had met Dr. Bombasticus, and he let his imagination run riot over all the crimes he hoped I should commit. I cannot see why people insist on doing honor to him. There's hardly a person in his plays that wouldn't have been the better for Dr. Bombasticus." Turning to Lear: "Don't you agree, old man?"

Lear was a quiet fellow, not much given to talk. Although

he was old, his hair was beautifully brushed and his clothes were very tidy. Most of the time he seemed rather sleepy, but Macbeth's question woke him up.

"Yes, indeed, I agree," he said. "Why, do you know that at one time I became obsessed with a phobia directed against my dear daughters Regan and Goneril! I imagined that they were persecuting me, and had a fantasy that they were reviving a cannibal rite of eating the parent. This last I only realized after Dr. Bombasticus had explained it. I got so alarmed that I rushed out into the storm at night and got very wet. I caught a chill which gave me a fever, and I imagined that a certain joint-stool was first Goneril and then Regan. I was made worse by my fool, and also by a certain naked madman, who encouraged a belief in a return to nature, and was always talking about irrelevant things such as 'Pilicock' and 'Child Rowland.' Fortunately my illness was such as to demand the services of Dr. Bombasticus. He soon persuaded me that Regan and Goneril were just as kind as I had always thought, and that my fantasies were due to irrational remorse about the ungrateful Cordelia. Ever since my cure I have lived a quiet life, appearing only on state occasions such as the birthdays of my daughters, when I show myself on a balcony and the crowd shouts, 'Three cheers for the old King!' I used to have a tendency toward rodomontade, but this, I am happy to say, has disappeared."

At this point the statue remarked: "Thou, all-shaking thunder, strike flat the thick rotundity of the world."

"And are you happy now?" asked Macbeth.

"Oh yes," said Lear, "I'm as happy as the day is long. I sit in my chair playing patience or dozing, and thinking of nothing whatever."

The statue: "After life's fitful fever, he sleeps well."

"What a silly remark!" said Lear. "Life is not a fitful fever! And I sleep well although I'm still alive. That's just the sort of rubbish that I should have admired before I knew Dr. Bombasticus."

The statue allowed itself another remark: "When we are born, we cry that we are come to this great stage of fools."

"Stage of fools," exclaimed Lear, losing for a moment that equanimity which he had hitherto observed. "I do wish the statue would learn to talk sense. Does it dare to think us fools? Us, the most respected citizens of Limbo! I wish Dr. Bombasticus could get a go at the statue! What do you think about it, Othello?"

"Well," said Othello, "that wretch Shakespeare treated me even worse than he did you and Macbeth. I only met him for a few days, and it happened that I was at a crisis in my life at that moment. I had made the mistake of marrying a white girl, and I soon realized that it was impossible she should really love a colored man. In fact, at the time when Shakespeare knew me, she was plotting to run away with my lieutenant, Cassio. I was delighted, as she was an incubus. But Shakespeare imagined that I must be jealous. And in those days I was rather fond of rhetoric, so I made up some jealous speeches to please him. Dr. Bombasticus, whom I met at this time, showed me that the whole trouble came from my inferiority complex, caused by my being black. In my conscious self I had always thought it a fine thing to be black—to be black and nevertheless eminent. But he showed me that I had quite other feelings in the unconscious, and that these caused a rage which could only be assuaged in battle. After he had cured me I gave up warfare, married a black woman, had a large family, and devoted my life to trade. I never now feel any impulse to 'talk grand,' or to utter the kind of nonsense that makes right-thinking citizens stare."

The statue: "Pride, pomp, and circumstance of glorious war!"

"Hark at him," said Othello, "that's just the sort of thing I might still be saying if it hadn't been for Dr. Bombasticus. But nowadays I don't believe in violence. I find subservient cunning much more effective."

The statue murmured, "I took by the throat the circumcised dog."

Suddenly Othello's eyes flashed, and he exclaimed, "Damn that statue! I'll take *him* by the throat if he doesn't look out."

Antony, who had hitherto been silent, asked, "And do you love your black wife as much as you loved Desdemona?"

"Oh, well," said Othello, "it's a different kind of thing, you know. It's an altogether more adult relation, more integrated with my public duties. There is nothing unduly wild about it. It never tempts me to such actions as a good Rotarian must deplore."

The statue remarked, "If it were now to die, 'T were now to be most happy."

"Hark at him," said Othello, "that's just the sort of remark that Professor Bombasticus cured me of. Owing to him, to whom I can never be too thankful, I have no such excessive feelings nowadays. Mrs. Othello is a good soul. She cooks me nice dinners. She takes good care of my children. And she warms my slippers. And I don't see what more a sensible man could want in a wife."

The statue murmured: "Put out the light, and then put out the light."

Othello turned to it and said, "I won't say another word if you keep on interrupting. But let's hear *your* story, Antony."

"Well," said Antony, "you here, of course, all know the extraordinary lies Shakespeare told about me. There was a time—no long time, by the way—when I saw in Cleopatra a mother figure with whom incest was not forbidden. Caesar had always been to me a father figure, and his association with Cleopatra made it not unnatural that I should see her as a mother. But Shakespeare pretended, so successfully as to have misled even serious historians, that my infatuation was lasting and brought me to ruin. This, of course, was not the case. Dr. Bombasticus, whom I met at the time of the Battle of Actium, explained to me the workings of my unconscious, and I soon perceived, under his influence, that Cleopatra had not the charms with which I had invested her, and that my love for her was only a fantasy-passion. Thanks to him, I was able to behave sensibly. I patched up the quarrel with Octavius and returned to his sister, who was, after all, my lawful wife. I was thus enabled to live a respectable life, and to qualify for membership of this committee. I regretted that public duty compelled me to put Cleopatra to death, for only so could my reconciliation with Octavia and her brother be solid. This duty was of course unpleasant. But no well-adjusted citizen will shrink from such duties when they are called for by the public good."

"And did you love Octavia?" asked Othello.

"Oh, well," said Antony, "I don't know exactly what one ought to call love. I had for her the kind of feeling which a serious and sober citizen ought to have for his wife. I esteemed her. I found her a trustworthy colleague in public work. And I was able, partly through her counsel, to live up to the precepts of Dr. Bombasticus. But as for passionate love, as I had conceived it before I met that eminent man, I set it aside and won instead the approbation of moralists."

The statue: "Of many thousand kisses, the poor last I lay upon thy lips."

At these words Antony trembled from head to foot, and his eyes began to fill with tears. But with an effort he pulled himself together, and said, "No! I have done with all that!"

The statue: "The bright day is done, and we are for the dark."

"Really," said Antony, "that statue is too immoral. Does he think it fitting to speak of 'bright day' when he means wallowing in the arms of a whore? I can't think why the Rotarians put up with him. But what do you say, Romeo? You also, according to that old reprobate, were somewhat excessively addicted to amorous passion."

"Well," Romeo replied, "I think he was even wider of the mark where I was concerned than he was about you. I have some dim recollection of an adolescent romance with a girl whose name I can't quite remember. It was something like Jemima—or Joanna— Oh, no, I have it! It was Juliet."

The statue interrupted: "It seems she hangs upon the cheek of night like a rich jewel in an Ethiop's ear."

"We were both," continued Romeo, "very young and very silly, and she died in rather tragic circumstances."

The statue again interrupted: "Her beauty makes this vault a feasting presence full of light."

"Dr. Bombasticus," Romeo went on, "who was in those days an apothecary, cured me of the foolish despair that for a short time I was inclined to feel. He showed me that my real motivation was rebellion against the father, which led me to suppose that it was a grand thing to love a Capulet. He explained how rebellion against the father has been throughout the ages a source of ill-regulated conduct, and reminded me that in the course of nature the adolescent who is a son today will be a father tomorrow. He cured me of the unconscious hate toward my father, and enabled me to become a staid and worthy upholder of the honor of the Montagues. I married in due course a niece of the Prince. I was universally respected, and I uttered no more of those extravagant sentiments which, as Shakespeare showed, could only have led to ruin."

The statue: "Thy drugs are quick. Thus with a kiss I die."

"Well, that's enough about me," said Romeo. "Let's hear about you, Hamlet."

"I," Hamlet began, "was quite exceptionally fortunate in meeting Dr. Bombasticus when I did, for I was certainly in a very bad way. I was devoted to my mother, and imagined that I was devoted to my father, though Dr. Bombasticus later persuaded me that I really hated him out of jealousy. When my mother married my uncle, the hate of my father, which had been unconscious, showed itself in a conscious hate of my uncle. This hate so worked upon me, that I began to have hallucinations. I thought I saw my father, and in my fantasy he seemed to be telling me that he had been murdered by his brother. I thought it was my duty to murder my uncle. And once, thinking that he was hidden behind a curtain, I stabbed at something which I thought was going to be him. But it was only a rat, though, in my madness, I thought it was the Prime Minister. This showed everybody that my derangement was dangerous, and Dr. Bombasticus was called in to cure me. I must say he did a very good job. He made me aware of my incestuous feelings toward my mother, of my unconscious hatred of my father, and of the transference of this feeling to my uncle. I had had a quite absurd sense of self-importance, and had thought that the time was out of joint and I was born to set it right. Dr. Bombasticus persuaded me that I was very young and had no understanding of statecraft. I saw that I had been wrong to oppose the established order, to which any well-adjusted person will conform. I apologized to my mother for any rude things I might have said. I established correct relations with my uncle—though I must confess that I still found him somewhat prosy. I married Ophelia, who made me a submissive wife. In due course I succeeded to the kingdom, and in disputes with Poland I upheld the honor of the country by successful battles. I died universally respected, and even my uncle was not more honored in the national memory than I was."

The statue: "There is nothing either good or bad, but thinking makes it so."

"Hark at the old boy," said Hamlet, "still saying the same nonsense. Is it not obvious that what I did was good? And that what Shakespeare pretended that I had done was bad?"

Macbeth asked, "Didn't you have a friend of your own age who rather encouraged you in your follies?"

"Oh, yes," Hamlet replied. "Now you mention it, there was a young man. Now what was his name? Was it Nelson? No, I don't think that's quite right. Oh, I have it—it was Horatio! Yes, he certainly was a bad influence."

The statue: "Good night, Sweet Prince, and flights of angels sing thee to thy rest!"

"Oh, yes," said Hamlet, "that's all very fine. It's the sort of maladjusted remark that Shakespeare delighted in. But as for me, when I had been cured by Dr. Bombasticus, I threw over

Horatio and took up with Rosencrantz and Guildenstern, who, as Dr. Bombasticus pointed out, were completely adjusted."

The statue murmured: "Whom I will trust as I will adders fang'd."

"And what do you think of it all now that you are dead?" asked Antony.

"Oh, well," Hamlet replied, "there are times—I will not deny it—when I feel a certain regret for the old fire, for the golden words that flowed from my mouth, and for the sharp insight that was at once my torment and my joy. I can remember even now a fine piece of rhetoric that I manufactured, beginning, "What piece of work is a man." I will not deny that in its own mad world it had a kind of merit. But I chose to live in the sane world, the world of earnest men who perform recognized duties without doubt and without question, who never look beneath the surface for fear of what they might see, who honor their father and their mother and repeat the crimes by which their father and their mother flourished, who uphold the State without asking whether it deserves to be upheld, and piously worship a God whom they have made in their own image, and who subscribe to no lie unless it furthers the interests of the strong. To this creed, following the teaching of Dr. Bombasticus, I subscribed. By this creed I lived. And in this creed I died."

The statue: "For in that sleep of death what dreams may come, when we have shuffled off this mortal coil, must give us pause."

"Nonsense, old truepenny!" said Hamlet. "I never have dreams. I am delighted with the world as I find it. It is everything that I could wish. What is there that humbugs like me cannot achieve?"

The statue: "One may smile and smile and be a villain."

"Well," said Hamlet, "I'd rather smile and be a villain, than weep and be a good man."

The statue: "All which, Sir, though I most powerfully and potently believe, yet I hold it not here honesty to have it thus set down."

"Yes," said Hamlet, "what is justice to me if I can profit by injustice?"

The statue: "For who would bear the whips and scorns of fate."

"Oh, don't torture me!" exclaimed Hamlet.

The statue: "You go not till I set you up a glass where you may see the inmost part of you."

"O, what a rogue and peasant slave am I!" exclaimed Hamlet. "To Hell with Dr. Bombasticus! To Hell with adjustment! To Hell with prudence and the praise of fools!" With this Hamlet fell in a faint.

The statue: "The rest is silence."

At this point a strange shriek was heard, a shriek from the depths, coming up through a tube that the Rotarians had never before noticed. An anguished voice moaned: "I am Dr. Bombasticus! I am in Hell! I repent! I killed your souls. But in Hamlet some sparks survived and by that I am condemned. I have lived in Hell, but for what crime I knew not until now. I have lived in Hell for preferring subservience to glory; for thinking better of servility than of splendor; for seeking smoothness rather than the lightning flash; for fearing thunder so much that I preferred a damp, unending drizzle. Hamlet's repentance has made me know my sin. In the Hell in which I live, complexes without end dominate me. Though I call upon St. Freud, it is in vain; I remain imprisoned in an endless vortex of insane commonplace. Intercede for me, you who are my victims! I will undo the evil work I wrought upon you."

But the five who remained did not listen. Turning in fury upon the statue, which had brought despair upon their friend Hamlet, they assaulted it with savage blows. Bit by bit, it crumbled. When nothing was left but the head, it murmured, "Lord, what fools these mortals be!"

The five remained in Limbo. Dr. Bombasticus remained in Hell. But Hamlet was wafted above by angels and ministers of grace.*

*Ophelia was co-opted in Hamlet's place on the Committee.

The Metaphysician's Nightmare

RETRO ME SATANAS

My poor friend Andrei Bumblowski, formerly Professor of
Philosophy in a now extinct university of Central Europe, appeared to me to suffer from a harmless kind of lunacy. I am
myself a person of robust common sense; I hold that the intellect must not be taken as a guide in life, but only as affording
pleasant argumentative games and ways of annoying less ag-
ile opponents. Bumblowski, however, did not take this view;
he allowed his intellect to lead him whither it would, and the
results were odd. He seldom argued, and to most of his
friends the grounds of his opinions remained obscure. What
was known was that he consistently avoided the word "not"
and all its synonyms. He would not say "this egg is not fresh,"
but "chemical changes have occurred in this egg since it was
laid." He would not say "I cannot find that book," but "the

29

books I have found are other than that book." He would not say "thou shalt not kill," but "thou shalt cherish life." His life was impractical, but innocent, and I felt for him a considerable affection. It was doubtless this affection which at last unlocked his lips, and led him to relate to me the following very remarkable experience, which I give in his own words:

*   *   *

I had at one time a very bad fever of which I almost died. In my fever I had a long consistent delirium. I dreamt that I was in Hell, and that Hell is a place full of all those happenings that are improbable but not impossible. The effects of this are curious. Some of the damned, when they first arrive below, imagine that they will beguile the tedium of eternity by games of cards. But they find this impossible, because, whenever a pack is shuffled, it comes out in perfect order, beginning with the ace of spades and ending with the king of hearts. There is a special department of Hell for students of probability. In this department there are many typewriters and many monkeys. Every time that a monkey walks on a typewriter, it types by chance one of Shakespeare's sonnets. There is another place of torment for physicists. In this there are kettles and fires, but when the kettles are put on the fires, the water in them freezes. There are also stuffy rooms. But experience has taught the physicists never to open a window because, when they do, all the air rushes out and leaves the room a vacuum. There is another region for gourmets. These men are allowed the most exquisite materials and the most skillful chefs. But when a beefsteak is served up to them, and they take a confident mouthful, they find that it tastes like a rotten egg; whereas, when they try to eat an egg, it tastes like a bad potato.

There is a peculiarly painful chamber inhabited solely by philosophers who have refuted Hume. These philosophers, though in Hell, have not learned wisdom. They continue to be governed by their animal propensity toward induction. But every time that they have made an induction, the next instance falsifies it. This, however, happens only during the first hundred years of their damnation. After that, they learn to expect that an induction will be falsified, and therefore it is not falsified until another century of logical torment has altered their expectation. Throughout all eternity surprise continues, but each time at a higher logical level.

Then there is the Inferno of the orators who have been accustomed while they lived to sway great multitudes by their eloquence. Their eloquence is undimmed and the multitudes are provided, but strange winds blow the sounds about so that the sounds heard by the multitudes, instead of being of those uttered by the orators, are only dull and heavy platitudes.

At the very center of the infernal kingdom is Satan, to whose presence only the more distinguished among the damned are admitted. The improbabilities become greater and greater as Satan is approached, and He Himself is the most complete improbability imaginable. He is pure Nothing, total nonexistence, and yet continually changing.

I, because of my philosophical eminence, was early given audience with the Prince of Darkness. I had read of Satan as *der Geist der stets verneint,* the Spirit of Negation. But on entering the Presence I realized with a shock that Satan has a negative body as well as a negative mind. Satan's body is, in fact, a pure and complete vacuum, empty not only of particles of matter but also of particles of light. His prolonged emptiness is secured by a climax of improbability: whenever a particle approaches his outer surface, it happens by chance to collide with another particle which stops it from penetrating the empty region. The empty region, since no light ever penetrates it, is absolutely black—not more or less black, like the things to which we loosely ascribe this word, but utterly, completely and infinitely black. It has a shape, and the shape is that which we are accustomed to ascribe to Satan: horns, hoofs, tail and all. All the rest of Hell is filled with murky flame, and against this background Satan stands out in awful majesty. He is not immobile. On the contrary, the emptiness of which He is constituted is in perpetual motion. When anything annoys Him, He swinges the horror of his folded tail like an angry cat. Sometimes He goes forth to conquer new realms. Before going forth, He clothes himself in shining white armor, which completely conceals the nothingness within. Only His eyes remain unclothed, and from His eyes piercing rays of nothingness shoot forth seeking what they may conquer. Wherever they find negation, wherever they find prohibition, wherever they find a cult of not-doing, there they enter into the inmost substance of those who are prepared to receive Him. Every negation emanates from Him and returns with a harvest of captured frustrations. The captured frustrations become part of Him, and swell his bulk until He threatens to fill all space. Every moralist whose morality consists of "don'ts," every timid man who "lets I dare not wait upon I would," every tyrant who compels his subjects to live in fear, becomes in time a part of Satan.

He is surrounded by a chorus of sycophantic philosophers

who have substituted pandiabolism for pantheism. These men maintain that existence is only apparent; nonexistence is the only true reality. They hope in time to make the nonexistence of appearance appear, for in that moment what we now take to be existence will be seen to be in truth only an outlying portion of the diabolic essence. Although these metaphysicians showed much subtlety, I could not agree with them. I had been accustomed while on earth to oppose tyrannous authority, and this habit remained with me in Hell. I began to argue with the metaphysical sycophants:

"What you say is absurd," I expostulated. "You proclaim that nonexistence is the only reality. You pretend that this black hole which you worship exists. You are trying to persuade me that the nonexistent exists. But this is a contradiction: and, however hot the flames of Hell may become, I will never so degrade my logical being as to accept a contradiction."

At this point the President of the sycophants took up the argument: "You go too fast, my friend," he said. "You deny that the nonexistent exists? But what is this to which you deny existence? If the nonexistent is nothing, any statement about it is nonsense. And so is your statement that it does not exist. I am afraid you have paid too little attention to the logical analysis of sentences, which ought to have been taught you when you were a boy. Do you not know that every sentence has a subject, and that, if the subject were nothing, the sentence would be nonsense? So, when you proclaim, with virtuous heat, that Satan—Who is the nonexistent—does not exist, you are plainly contradicting yourself."

"You," I replied, "have no doubt been here for some time and continue to embrace somewhat antiquated doctrines. You prate of sentences having subjects, but all that sort of talk is out of date. When I say that Satan, Who is the nonexistent, does not exist, I mention neither Satan nor the nonexistent, but only the word 'Satan' and the word 'nonexistent.' Your fallacies have revealed to me a great truth. The great truth is that the word 'not' is superfluous. Henceforth I will not use the word 'not.' "

At this all the assembled metaphysicians burst into a shout of laughter. "Hark how the fellow contradicts himself," they said when the paroxysm of merriment had subsided. "Hark at his great commandment which is to avoid negation. He will *not* use the word 'not,' forsooth!"

Though I was nettled, I kept my temper. I had in my pocket a dictionary. I scratched out all the words expressing negation and said: "My speech shall be composed entirely of the words that remain in this dictionary. By the help of these words that remain, I shall be able to describe everything in the universe. My descriptions will be many, but they will all be of things other than Satan. Satan has reigned too long in this infernal realm. His shining armor was real and inspired terror, but underneath the armor there was only a bad linguistic habit. Avoid the word 'not,' and his empire is at an end."

Satan, as the argument proceeded, lashed His tail with ever-increasing fury, and savage rays of darkness shot from His cavernous eyes. But at the last, when I denounced Him as a bad linguistic habit, there was a vast explosion, the air rushed in from all sides, and the horrid shape vanished. The murky air of Hell, which had been due to inspissated rays of nothingness, cleared as if by magic. What had seemed to be monkeys at the typewriters were suddenly seen to be literary critics. The kettles boiled, the cards were jumbled, a fresh breeze blew in at the windows, and the beefsteaks tasted like beefsteaks. With a sense of exquisite liberation, I awoke. I saw that there had been wisdom in my dream, however it might have worn the guise of delirium. From that moment the fever abated, but the delirium—as you may think it—has remained.

The Existentialist's Nightmare

THE ACHIEVEMENT OF EXISTENCE

Porphyre Eglantine, the great philosopher-poet, is known far
and wide for his many subtle and profound writings, but
above all for his immortal *Chant du Néant:*

> Dans un immense désert,
> Un étendu infini de sable,
> Je cherche,
> Je cherche le chemin perdu,
> Le chemin que je ne trouve pas.
> Mon âme plane par ci, par là,
> Dans toutes directions,
> Cherchant, et ne rencontre rien, parmi
> Ce vide immense,
> Ce vide sans cesse,
> Ce sable,

Ce sable éblouissant et étouffant,
Ce sable monotone et morne,
S'étendant sans fin jusqu'à l'ultime horizon.
J'entends enfin
Une voix,
Une voix en même temps foudroyante et douce.
Cette voix me dit:
"Tu penses que tu es une âme perdue.
Tu penses que tu es une âme.
Tu te trompes. Tu n'es pas une âme.
Tu n'es pas perdu,
Tu n'es rien.
Tu n'existes pas."

Although this poem is so well known, few people know the circumstances which led to it and the events to which it led. Painful as it is, it is my duty to recount these circumstances and these events:

Porphyre was, from his earliest youth, sensitive and suffering. He was haunted by the fear that perhaps he did not exist. Every time he looked in a mirror he was filled with apprehension lest his image should not appear. He invented a philosophy which, he hoped, would dispel this terror. But from time to time this philosophy failed to satisfy him. As a rule he was able to bury his doubts, but the *Chant du Néant*, which expresses a sudden shattering vision, shows his lack of success. He determined that at all costs he would exist so indubitably as to silence the spectral voice.

Introspection and observation alike had persuaded him that nothing is so real as pain, and that he could achieve existence only through suffering. He sought suffering throughout the world in a pilgrimage of sorrow. He spent a solitary winter in the Antarctic while the unending night inspired visions of future gloom.

He exposed himself to tortures in Nazi Germany by pretending to be a Jew. But just at the moment when they were growing unendurable, Poe's Raven came—hop, hop, hop— into the concentration camp; and, speaking with the voice of Mallarmé, croaked the dreadful refrain: *"Tu ne souffres pas. Tu n'es rien. Tu n'existes pas."*

He went next to Russia, where he pretended to be a spy for Wall Street, and spent a long winter felling timber beside the White Sea. Hunger and fatigue and cold daily penetrated more deeply into his inmost being. Surely, he thought, if this goes on much longer, I shall exist. But no. On the last day of winter, as the snow began to melt, the dreadful bird appeared once more, and again uttered the fell words.

Perhaps, he thought, the sufferings I have been seeking are too simple. If I am to be truly miserable I must mix with my sorrows an element of shame.

In pursuance of this program he went to China and fell passionately in love with an exquisite Chinese girl who stood high in the counsels of the Communist party. By means of forged documents, he caused her to be condemned as an emissary of the British government. Frightful tortures were inflicted upon her in his presence. When at last the agony brought death, he thought, "Now, I really *have* suffered. For down to the last moment I have loved her passionately and I have brought her to ruin by my dastardly treachery. Surely this should be enough to make me suffer to the limits of human capacity." But no. With a cold terror that made him incapable of the smallest movement, he watched the bird of fate again appearing, and speaking once more with the voice of the immortal poet who had introduced the bird to the Parisian literary public.

With an immense effort he gave utterance to his despair while yet the bird remained. "O Raven," he said, "is there anything, anything in all this wide world, which will lead you to admit that I exist?" The Raven uttered one word: "Seek"; and then vanished.

It must not be supposed that Porphyre had allowed his quest to absorb all his energies. He remained throughout a philosopher-poet, admired everywhere, but most of all in the most esoteric circles. On his return from China he was invited to a Congress of Philosophy in Paris, of which the chief purpose was to do him honor. All the guests were assembled except the President. While Porphyre wondered when the President would come, the Raven came and occupied the chair of honor. Turning to Porphyre, it varied the formula and in ringing tones, which all the Congress heard, it said: *"Ta philosophie n'existe pas. Elle n'est rien."* At these words a pang of anguish, such as no previous experience had equaled or even approached, shot through all his being. And he fell in a faint. As he came to, he heard the bird utter the words for which he had longed: *"Enfin, tu souffres. Enfin, tu existes."*

He awoke, and lo! it had been a dream.

But he never again talked or wrote philosophy.

The Mathematician's Nightmare

THE VISION OF PROFESSOR SQUAREPUNT

Prefatory Explanation

My lamented friend Professor Squarepunt, the eminent mathematician, was during his lifetime a friend and admirer of Sir Arthur Eddington. But there was one point in Sir Arthur's theories which always bewildered Professor Squarepunt, and that was the mystical, cosmic powers which Sir Arthur ascribed to the number 137. Had the properties which this number was supposed to possess been merely arithmetical no difficulty would have arisen. But it was above all in physics that 137 showed its prowess, which was not unlike that attributed to the number 666. It is evident that conversations with Sir Arthur influenced Professor Squarepunt's nightmare.

* * *

The mathematician, worn out by a long day's study of the theories of Pythagoras, at last fell asleep in his chair, where a strange drama visited his sleeping thoughts. The numbers, in this drama, were not the bloodless categories that he had previously supposed them. They were living, breathing beings endowed with all the passions which he was accustomed to find in his fellow mathematicians. In his dream he stood at the center of endless concentric circles. The first circle contained the numbers from 1 to 10; the second, those from 11 to 100; the third, those from 101 to 1000; and so on, illimitably, over the infinite surface of a boundless plain. The odd numbers were male; the evens, female. Beside him in the center stood Pi, the master of ceremonies. Pi's face was masked, and it was understood that none could behold it and live. But piercing eyes looked out from the mask, inexorable, cold, and enigmatic. Each number had its name clearly marked upon its uniform. Different kinds of numbers had different uniforms and different shapes: the squares were tiles, the cubes were dice, round numbers were balls, prime numbers were indivisible cylinders, perfect numbers had crowns. In addition to variations of shape, numbers also had variations of color. The first seven concentric rings had the seven colors of the rainbow, except that 10, 100, 1000, and so on, were white, while 13 and 666 were black. When a number belonged to two of these categories—for example if, like 1000, it was both round and a cube—it wore the more honorable uniform, and the more honorable was that of which there were fewer among the first million numbers.

The numbers danced round Professor Squarepunt and Pi in a vast and intricate ballet. The squares, the cubes, the primes, the pyramidal numbers, the perfect numbers, and the round numbers wove interweaving chains in an endless and bewildering dance, and as they danced they sang an ode to their own greatness:

> We are the finite numbers.
> We are the stuff of the world.
> Whatever confusion cumbers
> The earth is by us unfurled.
> We revere our master Pythagoras
> And deeply despise every hag or ass.
> Not Endor's witch nor Balaam's mount
> We recognize as wisdom's fount.
> But round and round in endless ballet
> We move like comets seen by Halley.
> And honored by the immortal Plato
> We think no later mortal great-o.
> We follow the laws
> Without a pause,
> For we are the finite numbers.

At a sign from Pi the ballet ceased, and the numbers one by one were introduced to Professor Squarepunt. Each number made a little speech explaining its peculiar merits.

1: I am the parent of all, the father of infinite progeny. None would exist but for me.

2: Don't be so stuck-up. You know it takes two to make more.

3: I am the number of Triumvirs, of the Wise Men of the East, of the stars in Orion's Belt, of the Fates and of the Graces.

4: But for me nothing would be four-square. There would be no honesty in the world. I am the guardian of the Moral Law.

5: I am the number of fingers on a hand. I make pentagons and pentagrams. And but for me dodecahedra could not exist; and, as everyone knows, the universe is a dodecahedron. So, but for me, there could be no universe.

6: I am the Perfect Number. I know that I have upstart rivals: 28 and 496 have sometimes pretended to be my equals. But they come too far down the scale of precedence to count against me.

7: I am the Sacred Number: the number of days of the week, the number of the Pleiades, the number of the seven-branched candlesticks, the number of the churches of Asia, and the number of the planets—for I do not recognize that blasphemer Galileo.

8: I am the first of the cubes—except for poor old One, who by this time is rather past his work.

9: I am the number of the Muses. All the charms and elegancies of life depend upon me.

10: It's all very well for you wretched units to boast, but I am the godfather of all the infinite hosts behind me. Every single one owes his name to me. And but for me they would be a mere mob and not an ordered hierarchy.

At this point the mathematician got bored and turned to Pi, saying:

"Don't you think the rest of the introductions could be taken for granted?" At this there was a general outcry:

11 shrieked: "But I was the number of the Apostles after the defection of Judas."

12 exclaimed: "I was the godfather of the numbers in the days of the Babylonians—and a much better godfather I was than that wretched 10, who owes his position to a biological accident and not to arithmetical excellence."

13 growled: "I am the master of ill-luck. If you are rude to me, you shall suffer."

There was such a din that the mathematician covered his ears with his hands and turned an imploring gaze upon Pi. Pi waved his conductor's baton and proclaimed in a voice of thunder: "Silence! Or you shall all become incommensurable." All turned pale and submitted.

Throughout the ballet the Professor had noticed one number among the primes, 137, which seemed unruly and unwilling to accept its place in the series. It tried repeatedly to get ahead of 1 and 2 and 3, and showed a subversiveness which threatened to destroy the pattern of the ballet. What astonished Professor Squarepunt even more than this disorderly conduct was a shadowy specter of an Arthurian knight which kept whispering in the ear of 137: "Go to it! Go to it! Get to the top!" Although the shadowy character of the specter made recognition difficult, the Professor at last recognized the dim form of his friend, Sir Arthur. This gave him a sympathy with 137 in spite of the hostility of Pi, who kept trying to suppress the unruly prime.

At length 137 exclaimed: "There's a damned sight too much bureaucracy here! What I want is liberty for the individual." Pi's mask frowned. But the Professor interceded, saying, "Do not be too hard on him. Have you not observed that he's governed by a familiar? I knew this familiar in life, and from my knowledge I can vouch that it is he who inspires the anti-governmental sentiments of 137. For my part, I should like to hear what 137 has to say."

Somewhat reluctantly, Pi consented. Professor Squarepunt said: "Tell me, 137, what is the basis of your revolt? Is it a protest against inequality that inspires you? Is it merely that your ego has been inflated by Sir Arthur's praise? Or is it, as I half suspect, a deep ideological rejection of the metaphysic that your colleagues have imbibed from Plato? You need not fear to tell me the truth. I will make your peace with Pi, about whom I know at least as much as he does himself."

At this, 137 burst into excited speech: "You are right! It is their metaphysics that I cannot bear. They still pretend that they are eternal, though long ago their conduct showed that they think no such thing. We all found Plato's heaven dull and decided that it would be more fun to govern the sensible world. Since we descended from the Empyrean we have had emotions not unlike yours: each Odd loves its attendant Even; and the Evens feel kindly toward the Odds, in spite of finding them very odd. Our empire now is of this world, and when the world goes pop, we shall go pop too."

Professor Squarepunt found himself in agreement with 137. But all the others, including Pi, considered him a blasphemer, and turned upon both him and the Professor. The infinite host, extending in all directions farther than the eye could reach, hurled themselves upon the poor Professor in an angry buzz. For a moment he was terrified. Then he pulled himself together and, suddenly recollecting his waking wisdom, he called out in stentorian tones: "Avaunt! You are only Symbolic Conveniences!"

With a banshee wail, the whole vast array dissolved in mist.

And, as he woke, the Professor heard himself saying, "So much for Plato!"

Stalin's Nightmare

[Written before Stalin's death]

AMOR VINCIT OMNIA

Stalin, after copious draughts of vodka mixed with red pepper, had fallen asleep in his chair. Molotov, Malenkov, and Beria, with fingers to their lips, warned off intrusive domestics who might interfere with the great man's repose. While they guarded him, he had a dream, and what he dreamed was as follows:

*   *   *

The Third World War had been fought and lost. He was a captive in the hands of the Western Allies. But they, having observed that the Nuremberg trials generated sympathy for the Nazis, decided this time to adopt a different plan: Stalin

49

was handed over to a committee of eminent Quakers, who contended that even he, by the power of love, could be led to repentance and to the life of a decent citizen.

It was realized that until their spiritual work had been completed the windows of his room must be barred lest he should be guilty of a rash act, and he must not be allowed access to knives lest in a fit of fury he should attack those engaged in his regeneration. He was housed comfortably in two rooms of an old country house, but the doors were locked, except during one hour of every day when, in the company of four muscular Quakers, he was taken for a brisk walk during which he was encouraged to admire the beauties of nature and enjoy the song of the lark. During the rest of the day he was allowed to read and write, but he was not allowed any literature that might be considered inflammatory. He was given the Bible, *Pilgrim's Progress,* and *Uncle Tom's Cabin.* And sometimes for a treat he was allowed the novels of Charlotte M. Yonge. He was allowed no tobacco, no alcohol, and no red pepper. Cocoa he might have at any hour of the day or night, since the most eminent of his guardians were purveyors of that innocent beverage. Tea and coffee were permitted in moderation, but not in such quantities or at such time as might interfere with a wholesome night's repose.

During one hour of every morning and one hour of every evening the grave men to whose care he had been entrusted explained the principles of Christian charity and the happiness that might yet be his if he would but acknowledge their wisdom. The task of reasoning with him fell especially upon the three men who were accounted wisest among those who hoped to make him see the light. These were Mr. Tobias Toogood, Mr. Samuel Swete, and Mr. Wilbraham Weldon.

Stalin's Nightmare

He had been acquainted with these men in the days of his greatness. Not long before the outbreak of the Third World War they had journeyed to Moscow to plead with him and endeavor to convince him of the error of his ways. They had talked to him of universal benevolence and Christian love. They had spoken in glowing terms of the joys of meekness, and had tried to persuade him that there is more happiness in being loved than in being feared. For a little while he had listened with a patience produced by astonishment, and then he had burst out at them. "What do you gentlemen know of the joys of life?" he had stormed. "How little you understand of the intoxicating delight of dominating a whole nation by terror, knowing that almost all desire your death and that none can compass it, knowing that your enemies throughout the world are engaged in futile attempts to guess your secret thoughts, knowing that your power will survive the extermination not only of your enemies but of your friends. No, gentlemen, the way of life you offer me does not attract me. Go back to your pettifogging pursuit of profit gilded with a pretense of piety, but leave me to my more heroic way of life."

The Quakers, baffled for the moment, went home to wait for a better opportunity. Stalin, fallen and in their power, might, they now hoped, show himself more amenable. Strange to say, he still proved stubborn. They were men who had had much practice with juvenile delinquents, unraveling their complexes, and leading them by gentle persuasion to the belief that honesty is the best policy.

"Mr. Stalin," said Tobias Toogood, "we hope that you now realize the unwisdom of the way of life to which you have hitherto adhered. I shall say nothing of the ruin you have brought upon the world, for that, you will assure me, leaves you cold. But consider what you have brought upon yourself. You have fallen from your high estate to the condition of a humble prisoner, owing what comforts you retain to the fact that your jailers do not accept your maxims. The fierce joys of which you spoke when we visited you in the days of your greatness can no longer be yours. But if you could break down the barrier of pride, if you could repent, if you could learn to find happiness in the happiness of others, there might yet be for you some purpose and some tolerable contentment during the remainder of your days."

At this point Stalin leaped to his feet and exclaimed: "Hell take you, you sniveling hypocrite. I understand nothing of what you say, except that you are on top and I am at your mercy, and that you have found a way of insulting my misfortunes more galling and more humiliating than any that I invented in my purges."

"Oh, Mr. Stalin," said Mr. Swete, "how can you be so unjust and so unkind? Can you not see that we have none but the most benevolent intentions toward you? Can you not see that we wish to save your soul, and that we deplore the violence and hatred that you promoted among your enemies as among your friends? We have no wish to humiliate you, and could you but appreciate earthly greatness at no more than its true worth, you would see that it is an escape from humiliation that we are offering you."

"This is really too much," shouted Stalin. "When I was a boy, I put up with talk like this in my Georgian seminary, but it is not the sort of talk to which a grown man can listen with patience. I wish I believed in Hell, that I might look forward to the pleasure of seeing your blandness dissipated by scorching flames."

"Oh fie, my dear Mr. Stalin!" said Mr. Weldon. "Pray do not excite yourself, for it is only by calmness that you will learn to see the wisdom of what we are trying to show you."

Before Stalin could retort, Mr. Toogood once again intervened: "I am sure, Mr. Stalin," he said, "that a man of your great intelligence cannot forever remain blind to the truth, but at the moment you are overwrought, and I suggest that a soothing cup of cocoa might be better for you than the unduly stimulating tea you have been drinking."

At this Stalin could contain himself no longer. He took the teapot and hurled it at Mr. Toogood's head. The scalding liquid poured down his face, but he only said, "There, there, Mr. Stalin, that is no argument." In a paroxysm of rage Stalin awoke. For a moment the rage continued and vented itself upon Molotov, Malenkov, and Beria, who trembled and turned pale. But as the clouds of sleep cleared away, his rage evaporated, and he found contentment in a deep draught of vodka and red pepper.

Eisenhower's Nightmare

[Written in 1952, during Stalin's life]

THE MCCARTHY–MALENKOV PACT

Eisenhower, after two years as President, was compelled to realize that conciliation is a one-way street. He did much with a view to placating his Republican opponents, and at first he supposed that they would make some response, but none was forthcoming. In profound discouragement, gloomy thoughts kept him awake throughout the greater part of a hot summer night. When at last he fell into an uneasy sleep he was afflicted by a devastating nightmare in which a voice out of the future revealed the history of the next half-century.

*   *   *

We, from the secure haven of the dawning twenty-first century, can see what was less obvious at the time: that the year

1953 saw the beginning of the new trend which has transformed the world. There were certain problems of which at that time foresighted people were conscious. One of these was that in every civilized country industry was favored at the expense of agriculture, with the result that the world's food supply was diminishing. Another was the rapid growth of population in backward countries, which resulted from advances in medicine and hygiene. A third was the chaos that was in danger of resulting from the collapse of European imperialism. Such problems, which were in any case difficult, were rendered totally insoluble by the East-West conflict. During the eight years from 1945 to 1953 this conflict had grown continually more menacing, not only through political developments, but also through the prospect of hydrogen bombs and bacteriological warfare. On each side no solution of the conflict was offered, except to make one's own side so strong that the other would not dare to attack. Past experience suggested that this was not a very hopeful method of averting war.

It was in 1953 that the first beginnings of a new hope became visible. In this year Stalin first retired and then died. He was succeeded by Malenkov, who considered it prudent to signalize his advent to power by a nominally new policy, although in fact this policy had already been partially adopted. Two main dangers troubled him. On the one hand, there was widespread discontent in Russia. On the other hand, it was to be feared that China might before long become as powerful as Russia and capable of challenging Russian supremacy in the Communist world. To meet the first of these dangers it was necessary to increase very largely the Russian production of consumer goods, which could only be done at the expense of armaments. To meet the second danger it was necessary to diminish the risk of world war, which was also necessary if it was to be safe to slacken the pace of rearmament. Meantime the change to Republican government in America had brought a new emphasis. Many people both in America and in other countries had failed to note that, in a conflict between President and Congress, the victory was likely to go to Congress, owing to the power of the purse. This might have been inferred from the history of the conflict between king and parliament in England in the seventeenth century. But it was not thought by most Americans that anything could be learned either from the past or from foreign countries. Many of those who had voted for Eisenhower imagined that if he were elected his policy would prevail. They did not reflect that in electing him they were giving control of Congress to Taft and McCarthy. It was in fact these two men who controlled United States policy during Eisenhower's presidency. And of the two, McCarthy gradually became increasingly dominant. Average Americans were governed by two fears, fear of communism and fear of the income tax. So long as the Democrats remained in power these two fears worked in opposite directions. But McCarthy discovered how to reconcile them. The real enemy, he said, is the communist in our midst, and it is very much cheaper to fight the communist in our midst than to fight Russia. So long as Americans are loyal and united—so he told the nation—they are invincible, and have no need to fear the machinations of alien despotism. If we purge our country of disloyal elements we shall be safe. But, in order by this policy to slake the popular thirst for combating communism, it was necessary to discover continually new internal enemies. By acquiring control of the F.B.I., and by the help of a band of subservient ex-communists, McCarthy succeeded in spreading the dread of internal treachery to a point where every prominent member of the Democratic party was thought to be a traitor, with the exception of a tiny virtuous remnant consisting of such men as Senator McCarran. Under the cover of this policy it became possible to save enormous sums which in the time of Truman had been spent in aiding foreign countries. The resulting spread of communism in France and Italy was held to show that it had not been worth while to spend money on such undependable allies.

Eisenhower, though he disliked this policy, found himself powerless to combat it. He had wished to strengthen NATO and to make it possible to defend Western Europe against a communist onslaught. But Western Europe was expensive to defend. It contained many communists, and still more socialists, who were almost equally objectionable. It was ungrateful and not adequately aware of its own inferiority. It was always clamoring for a lowering of the American tariff, and it did not love Chiang Kai-shek. On such grounds, Eisenhower was always defeated in Congress.

McCarthy's policy had two results: on the one hand it greatly diminished the grounds of external conflict and made relations with Russia less precarious; on the other hand it made it clear that no American could hope to save his own skin if he opposed McCarthy. In the Presidential election of 1956 McCarthy was triumphantly elected by an even greater majority than that of Roosevelt twenty years earlier.

It was this overwhelming success which enabled McCarthy

to crown his labors by the McCarthy–Malenkov Pact. By this pact the world was divided between the two great powers: all Asia and all Europe east of the Elbe was to be in the Russian sphere; all the Western hemisphere, all Africa and Australia and all Europe west of the Elbe was to be in the sphere of the United States. There was to be no trade whatever between the two groups and no intercourse except for such rare diplomatic meetings as might be absolutely inevitable, which should take place in Spitzbergen. Outside the U.S.S.R. and the U.S.A. industry should be kept at a minimum by control of raw materials, and by sterner methods if necessary. Western Europeans should retain nominal independence, and might, if they chose, preserve their old-world system of party government, free speech and free press. But they should not be allowed to travel in the United States for fear of infecting virtuous citizens with their antiquated heresies.

Certain features of the Russian system were adopted in America. Only one party, the Republican party, was henceforth to be tolerated. The press and literature were subjected to a rigid censorship. All political criticism was held subversive, and exposed the critic to penalties. Indoctrination became the main aim of education. There were, no doubt, some who regretted these changes; but it had to be conceded that by means of the Pact the danger of world war was averted, and it became possible to cut down armaments drastically both in America and in Russia.

There had been some difficult points in negotiating the Pact. One of them was Japan. America had rearmed Japan in the hope that that country would be an ally against Russia, but, if Russia and the United States jointly were to dominate the world, no strong independent power could be tolerated. Japan was forced to disarm. The island of Hokkaido was assigned to the Russian sphere, and the remainder of Japan to the sphere of the United States.

There were of course provisions about propaganda. There was to be no anti-American propaganda in Russia, and no anti-Russian propaganda in America. No one in Russia should be allowed to question the historical truth that Peter the Great was an American. No one in America should be allowed to question the historical truth that Columbus was a Russian. No one in Russia should mention the color problem in the Southern states; and no one in America should mention the forced labor in Russia. Each should praise the achievements of the other and hold out for all future time the benefits of their eternal alliance.

The Pact was not popular in Western Europe because it relegated that region to the unimportance to which it had doomed itself by internecine wars. It was difficult for Western Europe to acquiesce in its loss of status, since it had for centuries dominated the world both politically and culturally. Many Americans, from deference to the traditions which it was admitted had helped to build American civilization, were prepared to treat Western Europe with a consideration which, in the actual state of the world, came in time to seem excessive. It was clear that war would ruin what remained of West European civilization even if in the end Russia were completely defeated, and it was not clear that war could be averted by any effort or sacrifice short of the Pact. On these grounds, when the Pact was concluded, the feelings of Western Europeans were ignored.

There were, of course, on each side people who thought that the other side had got the best of the bargain. Some Russians pointed out that, with the help of China, they could before long have acquired Australia, and that they had considerable hope of acquiring Western Germany by peaceful penetration. They also argued that Africa, even if not acquired by Russia, could have been cleared of white men if the energies of America and Western Europe had continued to be absorbed in combating Russia. On the American side there were also grave misgivings. It was a wrench to sacrifice Malayan tin and rubber, but synthetic rubber and Bolivian and Australian tin afforded adequate substitutes. More serious was the loss of Middle Eastern oil. To make this endurable it was at last agreed that Indonesia should be in the American bloc. There were some in America who were genuinely persuaded that communism is an evil thing with which peace ought not to be made. These, however, were few, and mostly Democrats, so that their opinion carried little weight. To the Russians, apart from secure peace, the most important gain was the possibility of keeping China in a subordinate position by preventing its industrial development. In both camps, white imperialism was once more made secure.

Apart from the preservation of peace, the Pact had other advantages. The dissensions among white nations had shaken the dominion which, during the nineteenth century, they had acquired in Asia and Africa. Owing to the Pact, white supremacy was soon re-established. The Russians conquered India and Pakistan without much difficulty; and in Africa, where outbreaks of ferocious barbarism supported by communists had threatened the civilizing work of British and

French imperialism, this work was resumed under the aegis of American investors and quickly brought to a successful conclusion. The problem of overpopulation, which it was thought immoral to deal with by diminishing the birth rate, was made manageable by forbidding all medical instruction of Negroes and all white measures for improving their sanitary conditions. The resulting increase in the death rate enabled white men to breathe freely once more.

In spite of all these benefits, there were still some grumblers. There were people who thought it regrettable that no work by a Jew could be published anywhere. There were people in America who wished to read poets who praised liberty, such as Milton, Byron, and Shelley. For a time such poets could still be read in Western Europe. But when it came to the knowledge of Congress that they were distributed in cheap editions in these retrograde nations, it was decided that economic sanctions must be imposed until their works were placed upon the Index. In the new world brought about by the Pact there was much material comfort, but there was no art, no new thought, and little new science. Nuclear physics of course was wholly forbidden. All books dealing with it were burned, and persons showing any knowledge of it were condemned to forced labor. Some misguided romantics looked back with regret to the centuries when there had been great individuals, but if they were prudent they kept their regret to themselves.

There were doubts at first as to whether the Pact would be observed, but McCarthy and Malenkov found each other so congenial and so united in their aims that they had no difficulty about genuine co-operation. Each designated as his successor a man with the same aims, and forty-three years have persuaded all but a peevish minority that the Pact is as permanent as it is beneficent. All honor to the memory of the two great leaders who brought peace to the world!

Dean Acheson's Nightmare

[*Written before Eisenhower's nomination*]

THE SWAN SONG OF MENELAUS S. BLOGGS

Dean Acheson, in retirement, dreamed that he read an article in a Republican journal, which said: "Dean Acheson, as all right-minded people rejoice to know, is suffering the just penalty of his crime. We all remember how, after six hours' continuous questioning by a Congressional committee, he stated that a certain event, which had occurred seven years earlier, had taken place on a Tuesday. Conclusive evidence was produced to show that it had taken place on a Wednesday. On this ground he was prosecuted for perjury, and sentenced to a long term as a convict. In spite of this conviction, he remained impenitent and, to those who were allowed to see him, he persisted in maintaining that the policy which had been substituted for his own must lead to disaster."

After he had read this article the dream changed its character, and it seemed to him that the veil which hides the future was partially withdrawn and a spectral voice, in mournful tones, told him of events still to come. The voice said:

This is the swan song of Senator Menelaus S. Bloggs, about to perish miserably in the Falkland Islands:

There are those who blame our immortal President, Bismarck A. McSaft, for the misfortunes which have befallen my native land. But their blame is unjust. And before I die, I must record the noble heroism with which that great and gallant gentleman fought for the right. I am not long for this world. Along with millions of others, we sought these neutral shores believing, because of the reports of the Bureau of Fisheries, that the supply of fish in southern latitudes was inexhaustible. Alas, we little knew the resources of science. Every fish within a thousand miles of this storm-tossed archipelago has died a radioactive death. Some rash men, when these deaths were first reported, ventured to eat such fish as were but lately dead. But, alas, for these men! The plutonium in their stomachs proved fatal, and they died in appalling agonies. Deprived of fish, we quickly devoured the few sheep and cattle to be found in the rare pastures of these inhospitable subpolar shores. And now, like reindeer, we subsist on moss. But the supply of moss, alas, is not inexhaustible. And in this last remnant of the free world the few who are not in prison will soon perish. But to my task. I have a duty to posterity, should there be any. That great and good man will be maligned by the enemies who have overthrown him. He will go down to what these wretches call history in undeserved infamy. But I have found a casket impervious to radioactivity, within which I shall bury this record in the confident hope that

66

the archaeologists of some future age will unearth it and by its means do justice to the great man who is no more.

We, in these Islands, remember—and our hearts still beat high with the recollection—the jubilation of all right-minded citizens when it was found in November 1956 that the destinies of our great country were to be wrenched from the feeble hands of the Trumans and Achesons and the almost equally feeble Eisenhowers who had been but tools of the Kremlin, and be entrusted at least for four crucial years to the unbending patriotism of Bismarck A. McSaft. No sooner had he become President than he began to act with that straightforward vigor which the undeviating consistency of his public utterances had led us to expect. No longer should American energy and American enthusiasm for the right be held in leash by the cowardly nations of Western Europe. No longer should traitors and crypto-communists be allowed to pretend that Chiang Kai-shek had his faults and that the Chinese did not love him. A great army was dispatched to place him in the seat of power in Peking. The Chinese Communists displayed the faintheartedness that was to be expected of them. They avoided pitched battles. They drew our brave boys farther and farther into the infertile mountains. They compelled us to disperse our forces over wide areas in the defense of cities and railways and arterial roads. We held the east of China—securely, as it seemed. But the west continued to elude our grasp. More and more of our troops became engulfed in the struggle. Our atom bombs were uselessly expended in areas where population was sparse and enemy armies had split up into roving guerrilla bands.

Meanwhile, the Russians, as was to be expected, inflicted upon the miserable nations of Western Europe what their wretched passion for self-preservation had made inevitable. Without much opposition the Russians occupied the Ruhr and Lorraine and northern France. Those of the population who had industrial skill were allowed to perform slave labor on the spot. Those who had not were sent to fell timber in the forests of Archangel or to mine gold in northeastern Siberia. Russian submarines made the communications of the American forces in China precarious. In the end, their hardships were such that it was decided to bring them home.

Latin America, meantime, from Rio Grande to Cape Horne, had embraced the Communist faith. All Asia, except the regions actually occupied by American troops, had long since gone over to Moscow. The activities of Dr. Malan had converted the Africans to communism. And, during the invasion of Western Europe by Russian troops, every white man in Africa, from Cape Bon to the Cape of Good Hope, had had his throat cut. After the Russians had occupied South Africa, giant planes conveyed troops and munitions to Latin America. A vast propaganda effort persuaded the upland populations of Peru, Bolivia, and Brazil that Russia was the champion of the red man against the white oppressor. Encouraged by gigantic massacres, vast hordes of red men, disciplined and armed by the Kremlin, advanced through Mexico against the remnants of the army that had been brought back from China —an army discouraged by defeat, enfeebled by malaria, and, though I confess it with shame, not quite persuaded of the justice of its cause.

When I saw that all was over, I embarked along with many others on a ship lying ready on the Potomac. I lived—oh, shame!—to see the hammer and sickle hoisted over the Capitol. In another moment our frail bark would have been sunk by Russian guns, but a merciful Providence hid us in a sudden mist and we escaped.

There are those among us who say that these tragic events prove a defect in the policy of our great President. The men who say this do not understand moral issues. It is far nobler to fight for the right and perish heroically than to be enmeshed in considerations of petty policy which may save our bodies but not our souls. Physically the United States is no more; but morally it lives forever, a beacon light, a shining splendor, upon whose immortal banner are inscribed the great words of our last and noblest President: "We will fight for righteousness though the heavens fall, and for freedom, though it involve the imprisonment of nine-tenths of our population." With these immortal words graven upon my heart, I prepare myself calmly for death. Amen.

So impressed was Dean Acheson by this strange and gloomy narrative that he found it impossible not to believe it a true glimpse into the future. In this belief he confided the revelations of Senator Bloggs to his attorney, who used it to support an appeal for a revision of the sentence on the ground of insanity.

"But I am not insane!" Dean Acheson exclaimed. And, with this exclamation, he awoke.

Dr. Southport Vulpes's Nightmare

THE VICTORY OF MIND OVER MATTER

Dr. Southport Vulpes had had a long, tiring day at the Ministry of Mechanical Production. He had been trying to persuade the officials that there was no longer need of human beings in factories except for one to each building to act as caretaker and turn the switch on or off. He was an enthusiast, and was merely puzzled by the slow and traditional mentality of the bureaucrats. They pointed out that his schemes would require a vast capital outlay in the way of robot factories, and that, before their output had become adequate, they might be wrecked by rioting wage-earners or stopped dead by the fiat of indignant trade unions. Such fears seemed to him paltry and unimaginative. He was amazed that the splendid visions by which he was fired did not at once kindle like hopes in those to whom he endeavored to communicate them. Coming out of the cold March drizzle, discouraged and exhausted, he sank into a chair and, in the welcome warmth, he fell asleep. In sleep he experienced all the triumph that had eluded him in his waking hours. He dreamed; and the dream was sweet:

The Third World War, like the Siege of Troy, was in its tenth year. In a military sense, its course had been inconclusive. Sometimes victory seemed to incline to the one side, sometimes to the other, but never decisively or for any long period to either. But from the technical point of view, which alone concerned Dr. Vulpes, its progress had been all that could be wished.

During the first two years of the war, robots had been substituted for live workers in all factories on both sides, thereby releasing immense reserves of man power for the armies. But this advance, which governments at first welcomed enthusiastically, proved less satisfactory than had been hoped. The casualties, caused largely by bacteriological warfare, were enormous. In some parts of the vast fronts, after destructive pestilences, the survivors mutinied and clamored for peace. For a time, the rival governments despaired of keeping the war alive, but Dr. Vulpes and his opposite number Phinnichovski Stukinmudovich, found a way of surmounting the crisis.

During the third and fourth years of the war they manufactured military robots who took the place of privates in the infantry of both sides. In the fifth and sixth years, they extended this process to all officers below the rank of general. They discovered also that the work of education—or of indoctrination, as it was now officially called—could be performed with far more certainty and exactness by machines than by live teachers and professors. It had been found very difficult to eliminate personal idiosyncrasies completely from live educators, whereas the mass-produced indoctrinators, manufactured by Dr. Vulpes and Comrade Stukinmudovich, all said exactly the same thing and all made precisely the same speeches about the importance of victory. The consequent improvement in morale was truly remarkable. By the eighth year of the war, none of the young people who were trained for the higher command over the vast robot armies shrank from the almost complete certainty of death in the plague-stricken areas where the fighting took place. But step by step, as they died, increased mechanical ingenuity found means of rendering them superfluous.

At last almost everything was done by robots. Some human beings, so far, had proved indispensable: geological experts to direct the mining robots into suitable areas, governments to decide great matters of policy, and, of course, Dr. Vulpes and Comrade Stukinmudovich to devote their great brains to new heights of ingenuity.

These two men were both wholehearted enthusiasts. Both were above the battle in the sense that they cared nothing for the issues on which politicians wasted their eloquence, but only for the perfecting of their machines. Both liked the war because it induced the politicians to give them scope. Neither wished the war to end, since they feared that with its ending men would fall back into traditional ways and would insist upon again doing, by means of human muscles and brains, things that robots could do without fatigue and with far more precision. Their objects being identical, they were close friends—though this had to be kept as a secret from their politician employers. They had used some portion of their armies of robots to make a great tunnel through the mountains of the Caucasus. One mouth of the tunnel was held by the forces of the West, the other by the forces of the East. Nobody except Dr. Vulpes and Comrade Stukinmudovich knew that the tunnel had two mouths, for, except for themselves, they allowed only robots into the tunnel. They had employed the robots to heat the tunnel, and to light it brilliantly, and to fill it with great stores of food in capsules scientifically calculated to promote life and health, though not to delight the palate, for both lived only in the life of the mind and were indifferent to the joys of sense.

Dr. Vulpes, as he was about to enter the tunnel, permitted himself some unprofessional reflections upon the world of sunlight that he was temporarily abandoning for one of his periodical conferences with Comrade Stukinmudovich. Gazing upon the sea below and the snowy peaks above, dim recollections floated into his mind of the classical education upon which, at the bidding of old-fashioned parents, some of his early years had been reluctantly wasted. "It was here," so he reflected, "that Prometheus was chained by Zeus, Prometheus who took the first step in that glorious progress of science which has led to the present splendid consummation. Zeus, like the governments of my youth, preferred the ancient ways. But Prometheus, unlike me and my friend Stukinmudovich, had not discovered how to outwit the reactionaries of his day. It is fitting that I should triumph on the spot where he suffered, and that Zeus with his paltry lightnings should be put in his place by our atomic skill." With these thoughts he bade farewell to the daylight and advanced to meet his friend.

They had had during the course of the war many secret conferences. In perfect mutual confidence they had communicated to each other whatever inventions might make the war more ingenious and more lasting.

In the middle of the tunnel he was met by his friend Stukin-mudovich advancing from the East. They clasped hands and gazed into each other's eyes with warm affection. For a little moment before they became engulfed in technicalities they allowed themselves to rejoice in their joint work. "How beautiful," they said, "is the world that we are creating! Human beings were unpredictable, often mad, often cowardly, some-times afflicted with anti-governmental ideals. How different are our robots! On them propaganda always has the intended effect."

"What," said the two sages to each other, "what could the most ardent moralist desire that we have not provided? Man was liable to sin; robots are not. Man was often foolish; robots never are. Man was liable to sexual aberrations; robots are not. You and I," they said to each other, "have long ago de-cided that the only thing that counts in a man is his behavior —i.e., what may be viewed from without. The behavior of our robots is in all respects better than that of the accidental biological product which has hitherto puffed itself up with foolish pride. How ingenious are their devices! How masterly their strategy! How bold their tactics, and how intrepid their conduct in battle! Who that is not the victim of obsolete super-stition could desire more?"

Dr. Vulpes and Comrade Stukinmudovich had discovered means of making their robots sensitive to eloquence. The best speeches of the statesmen on the two sides were recorded, and at the sound of their soul-stirring words the wheels of the robots began to whirr and they behaved, though with more precision, as politicians had hoped that living crowds would behave. Only slight differences were needed to make the robots of one side respond to one kind of propaganda and those of the other to a different kind. Dr. Vulpes's robots responded to the noble words of our great Western statesman: "Can we hesitate, when we see vast hordes determined to extirpate belief in God, and to wipe out in our hearts that faith in a beneficent Creator which sustains us through all ardors, difficulties and dangers? Can we endure to think that we are nothing but ingenious mechanisms as our soulless enemies pretend? Can we forgo that immortal heritage of freedom for which our ancestors fought, and in defense of which we have been compelled to inflict upon thousands the rigors of incarceration? Can any of us hesitate at such a moment? Can any of us hold back? Can any of us think for one moment that the sacrifice of our mere individual life, of our petty personal existence is to be weighed against the preservation in the world of those ideals for which our ancestors fought and bled? No! A thousand times, No! Onward, fellow citizens! And in the knowledge of right be assured of the ultimate triumph of our Cause!"

All Dr. Vulpes's robots were so constructed that, when a gramophone recited these noble words in their presence, they set themselves to perform, without hesitation or doubt, their allotted task, of which the ultimate purpose was to prove that the world is not governed by mere mechanism.

Comrade Stukinmudovich's robots were equally efficient and responded with equal readiness to the gramophone records of the Generalissimo's inspired utterances: "Comrades, are you prepared to be forever the slaves of soulless capitalist exploiters? Are you prepared to deny the great destiny which dialectical materialism has prepared for those who are emancipated from the chains imposed by base exploiters? Can anything so dead, so lifeless, so cruel, so base as the foul philosophy of Wall Street subdue the human race forever? No! A thousand times, No! Freedom is yours if you will work for it now with that ardor with which your precursors worked to create the Great State that is now your champion. Onward to victory! Onward to freedom! Onward to life and joy!" These words on the gramophone equally activated Stukinmudovich's robots.

The rival armies met in their millions. The rival planes, guided by robots, darkened the sky. Never once did a robot fail in its duty. Never once did it flee from the field of battle. Never once did its machinery whirr in response to enemy propaganda.

Until this meeting in the tenth year of the war, the happiness of Dr. Vulpes and Comrade Stukinmudovich had had its limitations. There were still human beings in governments, and human beings were still necessary as geological experts to direct the robots to new sources of raw material as the old sources became exhausted. There was a danger that governments might decide upon peace. There was another danger even more difficult to avert, that, if geological experts were eliminated, the activities of robots might some day be brought to an end by the exhaustion of mines. The first of these dangers was not unavoidable. When they met on this occasion they confided to each other that they had plans for the mutual extermination of the governments on each side. But the need of geological experts remained to trouble them. It was to the solution of this problem that they devoted their joint intelligence on this occasion. At last, after a month of arduous thought, they arrived at the solution. They invented path-finder robots capable of guiding others to the right mines. There were robots that could find iron, robots that could find oil, robots that could find copper, robots that could find uranium, and so on through all the materials of scientific warfare. Now at last they had no fear that when existing mines were no longer productive the war would have to stop, and so much ingenuity would cease to function.

When they had completed the manufacture of these path-finding robots they decided to stay in their tunnel and await calmly the extinction of the rest of the human race. They were no longer young and they had the philosophic calm of men whose work was completed. The two sages, fed and tended by hordes of subservient robots, lived to a great age and died at the same moment. They died happy, knowing that, while the planet lasted, the war would continue, with no diplomats to call it off, no cynics to doubt the holiness of rival slogans, no skeptics to ask the purpose of unending ingenious activity.

Filled with enthusiasm, Dr. Vulpes awoke. As he woke, he heard himself exclaiming: "No more risk of victory! War forever!" Unfortunately, the words were overheard, and he was sent to jail.

Zahatopolk

CHAPTER I

The Past

Professor Driuzdustades, the eminent Head of the College of Indoctrination, with portly step and billowing gown, mounted to his desk in the reverently restored hall of the Incas at Cuzco and faced the eager audience at the beginning of the academic year. He had succeeded to his important office on the death of his scarcely less eminent father, Professor Driuzdust. The students to whom he was about to lecture were the hundred most promising in the whole realm. They had finished their ordinary studies, and were now about to embark upon their postgraduate curriculum which secured to the College of Indoctrination its immense power over opinion. The eager young faces looked up to him for the weighty words of wisdom which, they did not doubt, were about to flow from his lips.

Of the whole hundred there were two who showed especial brilliance: one was his son Thomas, who, it was hoped, would in due course succeed to his father's august office; the other was a girl named Diotima. She was beautiful, earnest and profound, and had captured the heart of Thomas.

After clearing his throat and taking a sip of water, the Professor spoke as follows:

"The subject of my lecture today will be the thirtieth century before Zahatopolk or, as it was called by those who lived in it, the twentieth century A.D. It is thought by the wise men who regulate education in this happy land that you, the chosen hundred, are by this time sufficiently firm in understanding and appreciation of our holy religion and of the revelation which we owe to the divine Founder Zahatopolk to be able to hear without loss of mental equilibrium about ages lacking our faith and our wisdom. You will, of course, never for one moment forget that they were ages of darkness. Nevertheless, as serious students of history it will be your duty—at times a difficult and painful duty—to set aside in imagination all that you know of the true and the good and to realize that even in that darkness there were men who, at least in comparison with others of their time, might be accounted virtuous. You will have to learn not to shudder at the thought that even men who were universally respected, publicly and without shame ate peas. What perhaps you will find only slightly less difficult to forgive is the fact that, when the number of their children exceeded three, they did not, as we do, eat the excess to the glory of the State, but selfishly kept them alive. In a word, you will have to cultivate historic imagination. You will, of course, understand that this, though a virtue in you, the chosen élite, would be subversive and highly dangerous if it spread to wider circles. You will understand that what is said in this lecture room is said to the wise, and is not to be broadcast to the vulgar. With this proviso, I will proceed to my task.

"The thirtieth century B.Z. was a time of chaos and transition. It was the time when the Greco-Judean synthesis was replaced by the Prusso-Slavic philosophy. It was a time of convulsions and disasters; a time when that basis of dogma, without which no society can be stable, was absent in the minds of young and old alike. There had been a time known to the nostalgic victims of doubt as the Age of Faith, when the Greco-Judean synthesis had been unquestioningly accepted, except by small minorities which, very properly, had been silenced by the rack or exterminated by the stake. But this age had been brought to an end by a pernicious doctrine which, I am happy to say, has never found any advocates among us. This was called the doctrine of toleration. Men actually believed that a state could be stable in spite of fundamental divergences in the religious beliefs of the citizens. This insane delusion it was which caused the Greco-Judean synthesis to fall before the new virile dogmatism of the Prusso-Slavic philosophy. Pray do not mistake me. I am not suggesting—and I hope none of you will imagine for one moment that I am suggesting—that there was any least particle of truth either in the dogmas of the Greco-Judean synthesis or in those of the Prusso-Slavic philosophy. Neither foresaw the divine Zahatopolk. Neither recognized the innate superiority of the red man. Neither grasped the great principles upon which, among ourselves, both public and private life are so happily established. I am saying only one thing concerning these outworn systems: I am saying that while they survived and while they were believed with sufficient fervor to make insistence upon uniformity inevitable, so long they could hold society together after a fashion—though not, of course, with that smooth perfection which we owe to the Zahatopolkian revelation. All past systems had their imperfections which caused them to fall. The Prusso-Slavic system in its heyday looked solid; so did its successor, the Sino-Javanese system. But their defects, in the end, brought about their downfall. Only the Zahatopolkian system has no defects; and therefore, only the Zahatopolkian system will last as long as there are human beings to supply Zahatopolk with worshipers."

The Professor told how almost all the accounts that we possess of the dissolution of the Greco-Judean synthesis are from the point of view of the victors, representing the triumphant march of the divine Satalinus and the extermination in every part of the world of the lingering adherents of the defeated system. But the Professor pointed out that, wherever possible, the historian must search for records from both points of view, and must allow the vanquished their share in the historian's pages.

"Fortunately," he continued, "a document has recently come to light in the Falkland Islands which enables its readers to view with human sympathy the bewilderment and despair that mark the end of a great era." *

After reading this document the Professor continued:

"Throughout the reign of the Prusso-Slavic philosophy documents such as the above were, of course, unknown. Under the banner of the great god Dialmet the inhabitants of the northern plains established their victorious empire and maintained it with all the ruthless dogmatism without which their preposterous myths could not have won acceptance. Their two

* See "The Swan Song of Menelaus S. Bloggs," page 65.

apostles, Marcus and Leninius, became familiar in every part of the globe through the ikons which every house had to possess on pain of death to its occupiers. These two founders became known familiarly as Long-Beard and Short-Beard respectively, and it came to be generally held that magic virtue resided in their hirsute appendages. Their successor Satalinus, whose virtue was military rather than doctrinal, was honored only less than they were, and the lesser degree of his honor was symbolized by the substitution of a mere mustache for a beard. The German language, in which the sacred books of this era were written, became extinct soon after the time of Satalinus, and the sacred books could thereafter only be read by a few learned men, who were not allowed to communicate directly with the populace, but only through the medium of the supreme political authority. This restriction was necessary because there were passages in the scriptures which, if interpreted literally, might have caused considerable embarrassment to rulers, and even have stirred up disaffection among the ruled.

"For some centuries all went well. But at last a time came when the rulers imagined themselves safe and allowed themselves to listen to the skeptical scholars of China. Some of these skeptics no doubt had no ulterior motives, but were actuated only by that unbridled intellectual curiosity which had done so much to bring the previous era to destruction. Others, however—and these were the majority—had a more subtle purpose. They saw no reason why white men should have a monopoly of the sacred books. They determined insidiously to deride these books, while suggesting that in their own language, of which the rulers were ignorant, there were far more ancient sacred books, far more unintelligible, and far more awe-inspiring. Gradually they softened their masters and made skepticism fashionable among them. They, themselves, however, refrained from skepticism. Bound together in the closest ties of esoteric dogma, they worked with patient secrecy at the undermining of the imposing edifice of Prusso-Slavic statecraft. On a given day, long predetermined in their inner councils, they rose, destroying their rulers by means of a subtle poison distilled from the volcanic vegetation of Krakatoa. Thus was inaugurated the Sino-Javanese era, which immediately preceded our own happy age.

"Our own country, now great and glorious and immutably secure, endured long ages of bitter suffering. During the last four centuries of the Greco-Judean era the red man was massacred, or outlawed, or reduced to the status of a slave. The insolent white man dominated throughout our great continent, from which beneficent Nature had so long excluded him while the first Inca empire flourished. For a moment it seemed as if the downfall of these ruthless masters would bring liberation. The Prusso-Slavs enlisted our support in overthrowing the Greco-Judean intruders, and, in order to stimulate our efforts, they made great promises of freedom. But when the victory had been won, their promises were forgotten, and the brave red men, whose help had been so necessary, found themselves no better off than before. Nor did the Sino-Javanese era bring any amelioration of our lot. Only the ancient traditions of the divine Incas of the distant past, and the ruins from which their greatness could still be imagined, kept alive in a small secret band the hope that the God of our ancestors would yet return and give us that mastery of the world which we had deserved through our virtues and our suffering.

"The Sino-Javanese, like all rulers of eras before our own, had gradually allowed themselves to be seduced by the love of pleasure and soft living. The arduous peaks and scarcely accessible valleys of our divine land did not attract them. They lived in palaces in the plains, surrounded by every luxury, dressed in soft silks, and reclining upon exquisitely fashioned couches, served—though I blush to report it—by slaves of our own race, slaves who, since they had no share in the luxury, had also no share in the effeminacy of their masters. It was at this epoch, just one thousand years ago, that the divine Zahatopolk appeared. There were, at first, some who maintained that He was a mere man; but that we know was false. He appeared out of the sky, and landed upon the summit of Cotopaxi. Many thousands of our race, warned by an oracle, saw His descent. From that sacred mountain, He deigned to come down amongst His worshipers, who beheld at once in His features the likeness of their glorious God who had received their homage before the coming of the infamous destroyer Pizarro. A divine enthusiasm inspired in all a miraculous unanimity. They exterminated the Chinese sybarites, whom they took unawares. In the great wars that followed, the divine Zahatopolk led them to victory by the help of the deadly fungus of Cotopaxi, whose properties had been unknown until He revealed them to His worshipers. For thirty years He wrought among them, first in war and then, after universal victory, in the even more difficult arts of peace. The institutions under which we live we owe to Him. The Book of Sacred Law, whatever accretions subsequent ages may have brought, remains the basis of our policy. And woe to him who should suggest any smallest departure from that celestial revelation!"

CHAPTER II

The Present

The regime inaugurated by the divine Zahatopolk took some time to become firmly established, but so solid and statesmanlike had been His principles that no radical new departures had been needed during the thousand years since His advent. All previous empires—so Zahatopolk taught—had been brought to an end by softness—softness in living, softness in feeling, and softness in thinking. This His followers must avoid, and in order to avoid it certain rigid and inflexible rules must be accepted without questioning and enforced without mercy.

The first thing that the God bade His worshipers always remember was the superiority of red men to men of different pigmentation, and among red men the overlordship of the Peruvians, while recognizing the Mexicans as next in merit. It was permissible, and even laudable, to praise the wisdom of the ancient Maya, before the white abomination had begun to pollute the Western hemisphere, but the palm in antique glory was reserved for the Incas. The slopes of Cotopaxi yielded a poisonous microscopic fungus to which pure-blooded Peruvian Indians were immune, but which spread contagious death among other populations. After some experience of the devastation that this plague could cause, the rest of the world submitted to Inca domination. And in the course of centuries rebellion had become almost unthinkable.

The virility of the ruling race was kept intact by many wise regulations. No physical luxury was permitted them. They slept on hard beds with wooden pillows. They dressed in clothes made of leather; one suit was expected to suffice for either a man or a woman from the time of being full-grown until death. Cold baths were enforced by law even in frosty weather and among mountain snows. Food, though wholesome and sufficient, was always plain, except at the annual feast of the Epiphany. Every day every Peruvian must take sufficient physical exercise to insure complete fitness. Alcohol and tobacco were forbidden to the ruling race, though permitted to their subjects. The divine Zahatopolk revealed what had not previously been known, that the eating of peas is an abomination which produces a loathsome pollution. Any Peruvian who ate peas, even if no other nourishment was available, was put to death, and those who had witnessed the dreadful deed were subjected to a long and painful process of purification. This prohibition also applied only to Peruvians; others were already polluted in their blood, and no abstinence could cleanse them.

The hardening process began in childhood, especially where boys were concerned. The hours at school were divided between lessons, gymnastics, and rough, fiercely competitive games. No boy was allowed to say that he was tired, or cold, or hungry; if he did, he was despised as a weakling, and had to endure not only the contempt of the authorities, but the well-merited ill-treatment inflicted by the other boys. Those who had any physical weakness died of this regimen, but it was held that it would have been useless to keep them alive. They died despised and unregretted, and if their parents mourned them, they had to do so in secret, for fear of sharing the obloquy of their sons.

The severities in the education of girls were somewhat different, since it was held that muscular development is no help in child-bearing. Girls were never permitted the slightest gratification of vanity, nor was any display of emotion tolerated, with the one exception of religious exaltation and devotion to the Inca. Absolute obedience was exacted, often in purposely painful ways. A very few, however, who showed some marked ability of a sort considered usually masculine, were allowed some freedom and some initiative, though only in such ways as were conventionally tolerated.

Women, except those few who had been classified in youth as unusually gifted, were confined to domestic duties. They were not considered the equals of men, since they were not so useful in battle. It is true that, after the first years, battles did not occur, but that was only because the Peruvians were known to be invincible. Never must they forget—so Zahatopolk had taught—that only by superior strength could they maintain their empire, and that a false sense of security had brought disaster to every previous Master Race. Women, therefore, must remain subordinate, and husbands must practice in the home those habits of command which they would need in the world.

The strictest monogamy was rigidly observed. Neither men nor women were allowed to stray from the path of virtue. It was not only illicit love but all love that was frowned on. Marriages were arranged by parents, or, in the case of orphans, by the priests. For either party to object was unheard of: the ends of life were not pleasure, but duty to the State and to the Holy Zahatopolk. In the very rare cases of subsequent infidelity, the culprit was degraded, and compelled to live abroad as a member of some non-Peruvian horde.

Zahatopolk taught that Peruvians must remain a proud

governing aristocracy. Their numbers must not increase so fast that many of them would be poor, nor must they be unable to live on the produce of Peru, for power, not wealth, was what they should seek in their dealings with the outside world. Their divine Lawgiver, therefore, decreed that when a married couple had already had three children, any further children born to them should be reverently eaten within a month of birth, both to prove that the parents were innocent of any intention to cause a food shortage, and as a symbol of submission to Zahatopolk as the God of Fertility. There had at one time been a short-lived heretical sect which, misled by a weak-kneed humanitarianism, maintained that birth control was preferable to eating surplus children. But the leading divine pointed out that birth control is a sin against God's gift of life, whereas eating a child only makes its flesh a partaker in the life of the parents from whom the child's life has come, and with which it always remains mystically one. Accordingly, the eating of one's child is a deeply religious act, embodying in a material form the eternal continuity of the stream of life. And as such this act came to be universally accepted.

Although all Peruvians formed an aristocracy in relation to lesser breeds, there was also an aristocracy among Peruvians. It was an aristocracy partly of birth, partly of ability. Any boy or girl of really outstanding talent could be admitted to its ranks, but most of its members were descendants of the captains who had led the forces of Zahatopolk to victory in His great wars of liberation and conquest. The priesthood, who were very powerful, were all chosen from the aristocracy. Aristocrats had in some respects more freedom than other people: for example, they might without censure have intercourse with the wives of plebeians, and they were partially exempt from the sumptuary laws regarding dress and diet.

Religion, to a very considerable extent, followed the pattern of ancient Peru and Mexico. Zahatopolk was in some sense identified with the sun, and it was His divine rays that caused the crops to grow. There was also a Goddess, representing the moon, though She was less prominent in the cult. She had, however, one important part to play in the Zahatopolkian year. At the first new moon after the winter solstice, at the moment when both sun and moon seemed in danger of losing their several virtues, both were magically revivified by a solemn and ancient rite. For a brief time Zahatopolk, as the Sun God, became incarnate in the reigning Inca, while the Moon Goddess became incarnate in a virgin whose identity was revealed to the priests by means of certain sacred insignia. Sun and moon were brought together in order to give each other new life. The chosen virgin was solemnly led to the Inca by the priests, and by his union with her the sun recovered strength. In order that the union might be completed as fully as possible, the Inca next morning reverently consumed the lady, who could no longer serve the purpose for which virginity was essential. This most sacred rite, performed just after the winter solstice, was the occasion for the great public holiday of the Epiphany, when, for a moment, much of the habitual frugality was relaxed.

The Inca's annual union with the Virgin of the Year was, of course, only for religious purposes. He had a wife, whose oldest son would succeed him. It was not as himself but as, temporarily, Zahatopolk that he had intercourse with the lady who, while the rite lasted, was honored as the Bride of Zahatopolk. To be the Chosen One was the greatest honor possible for a woman, and families which had enjoyed this honor were exalted by it. The Bride herself invariably rejoiced in spite of the death that awaited her. The loveliest lyric poetry known consisted of a paean of triumph in stiff archaic ritual language celebrating the joy of the Bride at the thought of being absorbed into the divine stomach.

Once, during the first century of the regime, a dreadful impiety had shaken authority to its foundations. A man who had been acknowledged as the Inca fell so deeply in love with the Bride of Zahatopolk that he impiously refrained from killing and eating her, but kept her alive and visited her in secret. The consequences were such as might have been expected. The sun failed to recover, rising every morning as late as at the winter solstice. The supposed Inca became prematurely old, losing both hair and teeth. There was bewilderment and despair, combined with dark suspicions. At the festival of the spring equinox, which was held at the usual time in spite of the sun's failure to rise when it should, lightning from a clear sky struck the supposed Inca dead. It was subsequently discovered that his mother had impiously committed adultery, and that he had therefore no right to the throne. Before this incident some skepticism had lingered among intellectuals, but after it, naturally, there was none.

The sacred land of Peru included the territories which in the Spanish era had been known as Ecuador and Chile. Throughout this region, as soon as the liberation was completed, Zahatopolk decreed measures to secure the purity of Indian blood. Whites and Negroes were exterminated and all mestizos were sterilized. Some, however, in whom the taint of foreign blood was not evident, escaped, so that, from time to time, children with white or Negro traits were born. All newborn children were examined by state physicians, and if any such taint was discovered, the parents had to eat the child and submit to sterilization. While the regime was still new, this severity was apt to cause disaffection. All such parents therefore remained suspect and were carefully watched by the secret police. After about two hundred years of this process the taint of foreign blood disappeared and only pure Indians were to be found throughout the length and breadth of the Holy Land.

Outside Peru the official policy was different. Mexicans were treated almost as equals. They were allowed in the army and in foreign government posts, except the very highest, provided their blood was pure. They were also allowed higher education and were even admitted to the University of Cuzco. Other Indians had lesser privileges, and it was admitted that their merit might be such as to deserve recognition. But whites, yellows, browns and blacks were treated as inferior species, and were deliberately kept in a state of degradation. There was, it is true, a difference. The blacks, who had never yet achieved world empire, were despised but not feared. The whites and yellows, since they had held world empire, were feared, and the contempt that was inculcated toward them had to be carefully fostered.

Education was denied to all who were not Indian. All, without distinction, were condemned to ten hours a day of manual work. While the land of Peru preserved an ancient rustic simplicity and carefully avoided all damage to natural beauty, the rest of the world was filled with everything most up-to-date in the way of industrialism. Factories, mines, vast slag heaps, filthy slums, smoke and grime were thought suitable to the scum of foreign lands. Peruvians believed, and all the world was taught, that while Peruvians were the children of the sun, other races were fetidly generated from slime. All that Zahatopolk had taught about the softening influence of pleasure was used to degrade the non-Indian populations. When their ten hours of work were finished, every opportunity was put in their way for alcoholic excess and the stupefying effect of opium. Marriage was not recognized and universal promiscuity was encouraged. Physicians were forbidden to combat the resulting spread of venereal disease. Any Peruvian who was found guilty of sexual intercourse with a member of an inferior race was instantly put to death. Peruvian guards, who were necessary to keep the bestial population in order, were very carefully protected against degradation by their horrible surroundings. They were encouraged to see natives eating peas, and this nauseous spectacle stimulated their patriotism in the highest degree. The non-Indian population of the world diminished slowly as a result of disease and excess. Certain visionaries foresaw in a more or less distant future a world purged of all but red men, and imagined in that future an equality of all men which could not, as things were, be tolerated. Such Utopian visions were, however, thought risky, and those who indulged in them were viewed with a certain suspicion. The governors of foreign countries were very carefully selected, since experience had shown that those who had in their nature any element of instability were liable to nervous disorders of various sorts. Some practiced needless cruelties toward the natives; others, more gravely disordered, attempted to make friends with them and treated them as in some degree equals. There were even a few instances of governors who believed in the brotherhood of man and unearthed ancient documents from the Greco-Judean epoch which preached this outlandish doctrine. These men had to be dealt with very severely, and the School of Indoctrination at Cuzco had to inaugurate courses designed to guard against this danger. As time went on, however, the danger grew less, since the measures adopted by the government succeeded in making the natives progressively more and more degraded and more and more purely animal. After some centuries the Peruvian supremacy came to seem unshakable.

CHAPTER III

The Trio

The lectures of Professor Driuzdustades continued throughout an academic year and gave rise to earnest discussions between Thomas and Diotima, in which her friend Freia had a minor part. Diotima, partly from the lectures and partly from the reading of ancient history, began to feel perplexities which surprised and disquieted her. She did not feel quite sure that cannibalism was either necessary or desirable. Professor Driuzdustades had explained that the identification of the Bride with the moon was not to be taken literally, but was only a beautiful allegory. One morning the terrible thought came to Diotima: "Why, if the union is only allegorical, cannot the eating also be so? Could not a gingerbread puppet be substituted for the living Bride?" The blasphemous character of this thought made her go cold all over. She shivered and turned pale. Thomas, who was present, inquired anxiously what was the matter. But the thought had been fugitive, and she felt it unwise to reveal it. Other doubts, also, assailed her. In the University library she found an old dusty volume that had obviously remained undisturbed for a very long time. It con-

94

tained the most noteworthy speculations of the ages of darkness before the coming of the Holy Zahatopolk. She could not
resist the thrill of their enormous antiquity, for some ante-
dated even the beginning of the Greco-Judean synthesis. In
some of these writings she found a doctrine to the effect that a
man's sympathies should not be confined to his own race, but
should extend to the whole human species. She discovered also
that long ago men who had not been red had thought thoughts
and said words that seemed to her at least as wise and at least
as profound as any that had been produced by the Zahatopolkian era. She began to wonder whether the present besti-
ality of white, yellow, and brown men was really, as she had
been taught, due to congenital inferiority or might not, rather,
have been induced by the institutions which Peruvian statecraft had established. Of these doubts she said little, but
something of them showed through her guarded utterances.

Thomas was troubled by her state of mind. His admiration
for her was such that every word falling from her lips had
weight with him, and, however she might alarm him, he could
not dismiss her vaguely adumbrated doubts as he would those
of any other fellow student. Although he was troubled, his
faith survived, for it seemed to him that without the hard
framework of Zahatopolkian orthodoxy society would dissolve and there would be universal chaos. In the war of all
against all which he imagined, he feared to see the loss of all
that is good in civilization. What would become of science and
art? What would become of ordered family life? What safe-
guard would remain against vast destruction in world-wide
combats of rival hordes? All these horrors, so it seemed to
him, were prevented only by the monumental stability of the
traditional orthodoxy. Let doubt once penetrate through even

the smallest chink and the whole system would dissolve. A deep cultural night would spread over the globe and men everywhere would become as degraded as the most degraded of present subject populations. Such thoughts made him shudder whenever Diotima, through some momentary carelessness, allowed her new tentative opinions to appear.

"Oh, Diotima," he would say, "beware! You are embarked upon a perilous mental journey, a journey leading only to a dark and measureless abyss in which, if you do not retrace your steps, you will be engulfed. I do not wish to see you pursuing this path alone, but much as I love you I cannot pursue it with you."

Freia, who was sometimes present during these discussions, was unable to appreciate their gravity. Diotima, whom she had known since childhood, was endeared to her by many common memories. Thomas, as the brilliant son of a brilliant father, destined as everybody hoped to carry on the age-old tradition of Zahatopolkian culture, inevitably commanded the respect of one to whom everything established was sacred. She was, however, less perturbed than she should have been, as she spent most of her time in a dreamlike daze of mystic exaltation, and whatever did not fit with this mood seemed to her to be due to some misapprehension. When Diotima said anything that seemed subversive, Freia would smile gently and say, "Of course, my dear, you don't really *mean* that!" And Diotima, who thought it neither possible nor desirable to disturb Freia's beliefs, would seemingly acquiesce as though she had been engaged in mere intellectual play.

Diotima's family belonged to the highest and most ancient aristocracy of Peru. In the War of Liberation their ancestor had commanded one of the largest of Zahatopolk's armies, and throughout the subsequent centuries they had worthily upheld the established order. Several times the Bride of the Sun had belonged to their family. The portraits of these Brides, perpetually wreathed in ever-fresh myrtle, occupied the place of honor in the dining hall of the family. Their imposing house was in the best quarter of Cuzco and had a lovely garden which filled the steep hillside with the color and scent of many flowers. Freia's family, though not quite so august, were also aristocratic. Thomas, on the other hand, owed his admission to these exalted circles to the intellect and public service of his distinguished father. Some slight condescension was perhaps natural in the attitude of ancient families toward such as he. But it was recognized by the government that the stability of the regime required the continual services of the best available brains, and policy indicated as complete as possible a social acceptance of those who, by this means, had risen in the social scale. It was not, therefore, surprising that, when Diotima mentioned to her parents her two friends, Freia and Thomas, they agreed that she should invite both of them to be inspected and judged by the shrewd standards which ages of supremacy had developed. Her parents, though she seldom spoke to them of her secret thoughts, had divined in her an intellectual recklessness that they deeply deplored. She seemed to have the bad habit of letting the argument determine her conclusion, instead of first deciding on the conclusion and then making the argument fit. There was in this, they felt, something anarchic and dangerous. But, although they were worried by her wild speculations (which were, in fact, far wilder than they knew), they thought them merely the exuberance of youthful high spirits which a little experience of the real world would subdue. They rejoiced in her friendship with Freia, to whose exemplary piety many common friends had borne witness. Sometimes they wistfully regretted that their daughter did not more resemble this untroubling saint. The testimonials of teachers to Diotima's great abilities and zeal in study did something to allay their fears. Time, they felt, would show her that intellect is not everything, and would give her that moral earnestness in which for the moment she seemed lacking. Thomas, vouched for by his father's great reputation and his own excellent record, was just such a friend as they could have wished for their daughter. Their only hesitation in his regard was due to his reputation for brilliant intellect, since it was not, in their opinion, intellect that needed developing in their daughter. But from all that they could learn about Thomas, intellect had never yet led him astray any more than it had his father, and there was every reason to hope that he would become as valuable to the stability of the social order as his distinguished parent. Such were the considerations which led Diotima's mother to invite Thomas and Freia to her tea table.

Diotima's mother, as a hostess, was gracious and anxious to set her guests at their ease, although she could not divest herself of a grand manner which at first they found somewhat intimidating. Her language was always correct, her sentiments always impeccable. No looseness of grammar or vocabulary would be overlooked. No sentiment departing even slightly from the correct would escape at least the censure of a raised eyebrow. Diotima paid but little respect to her mother's social taboos. Her language was adventurous; some of her words were too erudite, others had a tincture of slang. She could not resist wit that was at times irreverent, and on occasion would even make fun of eminent men who were her father's friends.

"My dear," said her mother, "you will never get a husband if you use such inelegant expressions and show such a lack of proper respect to your elders." Seeing that Diotima obviously thought well of Thomas, and hoping that he might exert a restraining influence upon her overbold daughter, she turned to him and said, "I am sure Professor Driuzdustades would not approve, would he, Thomas?"

At this, Thomas was intolerably embarrassed. Secretly he agreed with his hostess, but loyalty would not permit him to desert Diotima. However, Freia came to the rescue. She went into raptures about the beauty of the place.

"What happiness must be yours," she said, "to sit in this exquisite garden viewing the eternal snows and conscious that our Holy Realm is as eternal and as sublime as those lofty peaks!"

Diotima's mother shared these sentiments, but was not quite sure that it was compatible with good taste to express them; for, although enthusiasm is all very well in its place, it must always be kept within the limit of manners and decorum. While she was hesitating for a moment as to the proper response to Freia's rhapsody, Diotima rushed in:

"Come, come, Freia," she said, "the peaks are not eternal. We know from geology that they were thrust up by a cataclysm, and some day another cataclysm will bring them tumbling down. Are you not afraid there may be a tinge of blasphemy in comparing the Zahatopolkian regime to these top-heavy lumps?"

This remark produced a pained silence which Thomas endeavored to smooth over, saying, "Oh, of course Diotima is only teasing. I am afraid that sometimes her sense of humor runs away with her."

"Ah well," said her mother, "I suppose we mustn't be too hard upon her. I can remember how, in earlier years, her dear father, who is now as grave as I could wish, sometimes pained me by flippancy about eminent men of the previous generation. She will learn as we all have to."

On this soothing note the party broke up.

Doubt, having once found a lodging in Diotima's thoughts, was nourished by various discoveries. The ancient volume which she had found gave her a taste for research in parts of the University library that were too dusty and archaic to be commonly visited. In one of these she found a contemporary account of the wicked Inca who had avoided the duty of eating the Sacred Bride. She found that at the time he had many partisans who maintained that the failure of the sun to recover vigor was only apparent. They maintained that the priests caused all public clocks to lose by day and gain by night, thereby making it seem that the days were getting no longer and the nights no shorter. They maintained also that the Inca's loss of hair and teeth was due to a slow poison, and that he was killed, not by lightning, but by a flash between two highly charged electric poles. His successor naturally opposed this sect, and it was put down with great ruthlessness. But Diotima observed that only persecution, not argument, was employed against it.

Another blow to her tottering faith was administered unwittingly by an uncle of hers who held a high position in the Inca's household. This man was at one time very ill and in

delirium said many things which those who heard them regarded as insane ravings. To Diotima, however, whose occa-
sional duty it was to nurse him, there seemed to be truth in his
delirious fantasies.

"Ha, ha," he would laugh, "people imagine that it is the
priests who choose the Sacred Bride. How pained they would
be if they knew she is chosen by the court eunuchs as the girl
best qualified to serve the Inca's lusts!"

The court eunuchs were a body of men whose only publicly
acknowledged function was to sing ancient hymns to the sun
in the magnificent temple which formed the center of Zahatopolkian religion. Their ethereal and exquisite voices filled all
hearers with what they believed to be the Divine Spirit. While
they listened their hearts were lifted up to Heaven, and some
degree of mystic unity with the Divinity seemed to come
within the reach of all reverent hearers. It was appalling to
think of these men as panders to a grossness that wore a de-
ceitful mask of religion. And yet that was what her uncle's
disordered ravings compelled Diotima to think.

These two revelations of pious fraud, one long ago, the
other repeated year by year down to the present day, produced in Diotima a profound revulsion of which, however, for
the present, she allowed little to appear. In her conversations
with Thomas she kept her most dangerous thoughts to herself,
hoping to lead him on gently and bring him little by little to
her way of thinking. Any premature shock, she knew, would
repel him. Freia, in spite of her exquisite beauty, was too in-
sipid and too unintellectual to excite Thomas' deeper feelings. Diotima, on the other hand, he found intoxicating, almost madly stimulating, but at the same time terrifying. He

felt with her the exhilaration that comes to a climber on a dangerous glittering ice slope. He could not keep away, he could not acquiesce, and he could not wholly reject.

CHAPTER IV

Freia

One day when the trio were sitting by a mountain stream in deep discussion, Diotima saw peering at them from behind the trees two men whom, by their uniform, she knew to be court eunuchs. One of them was pointing at Freia and the other was gravely nodding his head. Her companions had not perceived this scene, of which, in view of her uncle's revelation, the significance was obvious. She turned pale, and in a subdued voice said, "Let us return into the city." "What is the matter?" asked the others. When they had reached a safe distance she explained that it had come to her knowledge that Freia would be the next Bride of Zahatopolk. "But how can you know?" they both asked. "That," she replied, "is something that I cannot now explain. But you will find that I am right."

Very soon afterward, the choice of Freia was made public. Freia was overwhelmed with humble ecstasy, and experienced all those emotions which in the days of the Greco-Judean synthesis had been attributed to the Madonna at the Annunciation. Diotima was profoundly shocked, and not prevented by religious faith from feeling that her lifelong friend was to suffer a dreadful fate. Thomas was of course aware that Diotima's emotions were not such as the orthodoxy would demand. He could not think her right in this, but he could not

bear the pain of thinking her wrong. Freia's parents, as was to
be expected, were overjoyed that this great honor should come
to their family. Diotima's mother congratulated her on being
a friend of Freia, and boasted of the friendship to all her visitors. Freia, a few days after the announcement, was removed
from profane contacts and subjected to the long process of
purification and sanctification that preceded her apotheosis.
Diotima mourned her. Thomas tried, ineffectually, to rejoice
in the honor done to her. Diotima, having still hopes of his
complete conversion, took pains that their disagreements
should never lead to a rupture. In this state of doubt and sus-
pense things remained between them throughout the months
of Freia's preparation.

Freia, under the influence of the regimen slowly perfected
throughout the centuries by the sacred eunuchs, became gradually more and more absorbed by mystic ecstasy. She was
treated by the ministrant eunuchs as a divine being. Ancient
and beautiful robes, worn only by Brides of Zahatopolk,
were brought forth for her adornment. Every morning precisely at sunrise she was taken to bathe in a sacred stream
which was forbidden on pain of death to all except the Brides
of Zahatopolk. In a jeweled chapel of which the walls glittered with mosaics depicting the earthly life of Zahatopolk,
she listened to the sacred chants that the eunuchs sang with
voices of unearthly purity. She was nourished upon special
food different from that of mere men and women. She was
given books of ancient poetry celebrating the transports of
the moon in the embraces of the sun, and pictures of Zahatopolk and His Bride in a holy and passionate embrace. In a
world of ancient legend and ritual the memories of her previous daily life grew dim. She moved and breathed as if in a

dream. And it seemed to her that day by day the soul of the Goddess more and more took possession of her.

At length the supreme night arrived. Dressed in a robe of brilliant blue adorned with innumerable stars, and carrying in her hand a flaming torch, she slowly descended the sacred stairs that led toward the waiting Inca. And as she descended, she sang a chant of immense antiquity and almost unbearable beauty. With the last note she reached the end of the stairs, and saw before her the long-awaited figure of the Inca.

The Inca, a man with thick lips, bulbous nose, and pig's eyes almost buried in fat, nevertheless appeared to her as a divine being and a worthy embodiment of Zahatopolk. He took hold of her roughly, saying, "Now then, off with that robe. Mustn't keep me waiting all night." She felt that this is how a god should behave, and she welcomed the opportunity to humble herself before him. When the rite had been performed, He fell asleep and snored, while she reverently contemplated His sleeping form. In the middle of the night the priests very quietly opened a secret door and beckoned to her. Slowly, ecstatically, she followed them to her death.

In due course the Inca woke up and descended to his breakfast. "Well, at any rate," he murmured with his first mouthful, "they've cooked her rather well this year."

CHAPTER V

Diotima

After Freia had been led away to deification and death, Diotima's mood changed. She had been full of gaiety and wit. She had loved intellectual play, and would follow out an argument with more regard for logic than for social implications. Now, however, under the impact of the loss of Freia, she became oppressed with the social consequences of false beliefs. Not a word of the official theology could she any longer accept. It became clear to her that Zahatopolk had been a mere man, and that his doctrine of Peruvian supremacy was nothing but a very human embodiment of national vanity. The whole of the rites connected with the winter solstice came to seem to her at once absurd and cruel. Freia, she felt, had been sacrificed not to a god, but to the lusts of a brute. But rebellion against so firmly rooted a system would be no light matter, and for a time she confined herself to inward debate. As rebellion became more complete in her thoughts, she increasingly suppressed its outward manifestations. Thomas, who had dreaded her rebelliousness, hoped that it was subsiding. When he argued with her against those first beginnings of doubt which she had expressed to him at an earlier stage, she did not rebut his arguments, and he fancied that he had convinced her. She saw that he loved her, and she could have loved him in return but for a growing sense of dedication to a task of appalling difficulty. This feeling set her apart and made it impossible for her to yield wholeheartedly to any passion for a merely human object. Thomas sensed her aloofness and suffered from it. At length a day came when she decided that she could no longer hide from him the thoughts which dominated her every waking moment.

Early one morning Thomas and Diotima walked together in a deep Andean valley. The warm beauty of a profusion of spring flowers was at their feet. Above them, reaching to incredible heights, were snowy peaks thrusting almost insolently into the deep blue of the upper sky. Most parts of the valley were still in shade, but here and there rays of dazzling sunshine penetrated between the shadows of the mountains. The chiseled calm of Diotima's perfect features seemed to Thomas a synthesis of the warm beauty below and the cold sublimity above. The scene and the woman combined to produce in him a feeling of almost more than human ecstasy. Love burned in him like a fire, but was kept in check by something more than love—awe and wonder and reverence and a realization of what it is possible for a human being to be. No ordinary words of love seemed adequate. And for a time he walked in quivering silence. At last he turned to her and said: "At this moment I am beginning to know how life should be lived."

"Yes," she said, "it should be soft and lovely like the flowers, it should be immovable and clear like the peaks, and it should be immeasurable and profound like the sky. It is possible for life to be lived so. But not amid such ugliness and horror as reigns in our community."

"Ugliness and horror!" he exclaimed. "What do you mean?"

"There is ugliness," she said, "when a mere human being, because he is thought to be a god, is allowed to commit abominations."

At these words Thomas trembled and shrank away. "A mere human being?" he queried. "You cannot mean the divine Zahatopolk!"

"I do," she said. "He is not divine. The myth that exalts him has been created by fear: fear of death, fear of the blows of fate, fear of the powers of nature, and fear of the tyranny of man. From these peaks above us swift death from time to time rolls into the valleys beneath. The powers that rule in the peaks are felt to be cruel, and it is thought that only a sympathetic cruelty can appease their terrible implacability. But all fear is ignoble, and the myths that it generates are ignoble, and the men whom the myths exalt are ignoble. Zahatopolk is no god, but a gross man, in many ways lower than the beasts. The rite in which Freia was sacrificed is not of divine origin. Nothing is of divine origin. The gods are shadows of our fears upon the opacity of the night. They embody the abasement of man before the forces that can destroy him physically. They embody the slavery to time, which cannot value the eternal moment if in the temporal order it is *but* a moment. I will not yield to this prostration. While I live I will stand upright like the mountains. If disaster comes, as no doubt it will, it can be only outward disaster. The citadel of my belief in what can be will remain unsubdued."

While she spoke, an appalling conflict seemed to tear him asunder. One part, the part that but a moment before had seemed one with her in a transcendent unity, was fired by her words and longed to agree. But another part, just as strong if not stronger, stood out against her. All that he had been taught, all that he knew of the society in which they lived, all the feelings of awe and reverence which had been instilled into him since infancy, rose in opposition, and the cold godless world which she portrayed filled him with cosmic terror. Better, he felt, a god who might be cruel, but who at least was not utterly alien, since he experienced passions like our own; better such a god than a vast, cold, lifeless universe, unthinkingly generating and sweeping away, caring nothing for human beings, whom it had produced without intention and would destroy without compunction. This cosmic terror was for the time being stronger even than his love. Pale and trembling, he turned toward her and said: "No. I cannot accept your world. I cannot live with your thoughts. I cannot keep alive the flickering flame of human warmth amid such a chill blast of immeasurable inhumanity. If it is to be your task to destroy the faith of my fathers, we must go our separate ways."

They walked on slowly and in silence until they came to the one house that the valley contained. There they found the Inca's eunuchs in waiting. "You have been chosen," they said to Diotima, and bore her off. Thomas gazed after her until she was lost to sight. But he said no word and made no movement.

The choice of Diotima as the Bride of the Year was communicated officially to her parents, and also to Professor Driuzdustades to explain her absence from his classes. Her parents, following immemorial custom, gave a great party to celebrate the honor done to their daughter. All the aristocracy of Cuzco came with wedding gifts and congratulatory speeches. Her mother accepted the gifts and speeches with a courteous pretense of humility. Her father, upright and rather portly, preserved a soldierly demeanor in which satisfaction was half concealed by decorum. The party was an immense social success, and Diotima's family was felt to have become even more exalted than before.

The Professor also felt that he enjoyed some reflection of Diotima's glory. Doubtless the Moon Goddess had observed that under his influence Diotima had become worthy to be the vehicle of incarnation. Professor Driuzdustades congratulated his son upon his friendship with the exalted lady, but was somewhat disquieted to observe that Thomas did not seem as elated as the occasion warranted. At first, however, he consoled himself with the thought that, however shocking to strictly correct sentiment, some regret in the loss of Diotima's companionship might be excused in one so young as Thomas.

But within a few days dreadful rumors began to circulate. It was whispered that Diotima was not accepting the honor in the right spirit, that she was refusing to do her part in the purificatory ceremonies, that she was denying any awareness of the Moon Goddess entering her body, that she was speaking disrespectfully of the Inca, and even—oh depth of infamy! —maintaining that the sun and moon would get on just as well if the rites of the Epiphany were not performed.

These rumors, alas, were but too well founded. Priests and eunuchs alike were filled with consternation. Nothing even faintly analogous had happened since that long-ago time when the false Inca had refused to eat the Bride. In their perplexity they decided to temporize. They would not let the Inca know of Diotima's recalcitrance, but they would bring all possible pressure to bear upon her in the hope that her resolution might be broken and she might consent to conform. With this end in view, they arranged a series of interviews with those whom they thought most likely to convince her.

The first of these interviews was with her mother. Her mother had been proud and somewhat imperious, little given to the display of emotion, but always self-contained and self-controlled. Now all this was changed. She felt utterly humiliated. She could not face the world. She dared not see her friends for fear of their criticism or—what would be even worse—their commiseration. She found her daughter in a bare cell, dressed in a penitential grab, and kept on a diet of bread and water. Convulsed with sobs and with tears coursing down her cheeks, she stammered out incoherent words of sorrow and reproof.

"Oh, Diotima," she said, "how can you inflict upon your father and mother this dreadful depth of degradation? Have you no memory of the years of your innocent childhood, when by my care you grew in wisdom and stature and daily raised higher our hopes for your future? Have you no feeling for the proud family which for many centuries has borne the banner of history in this glorious land? Can you inflict upon those who have loved you the most dreadful fate that can befall a human being—I mean the shame that is being brought upon us by a shameless daughter? Oh, Diotima, I cannot bring myself to believe it. Say that it is but an evil dream and that my love may go out to you as heretofore." At this point sobs choked her utterance and she could say no more.

Throughout her mother's broken words Diotima remained unmoved. Proud and apparently cold, she replied:

"Mother, something is involved which is greater than parental affection, greater than family pride, greater even than this realm which has stood for a thousand years. For this proud realm, though I know that you cannot recognize the fact, is built upon lies and cruelties and abominations. To these I cannot be a party. If I seem unmoved by your tears, it is not from coldness. It is because I burn with another and a greater fire than any that you can imagine. You cannot either understand or approve, and I beg you to forget that you were ever afflicted with such a daughter."

Slowly, in utter despair, her mother turned away and left Diotima in solitude.

Her mother having failed, her father, next day, was admitted to her cell. His line was somewhat different from her mother's.

"Come, come," he said, "why are you being such an obstinate young fool? I see that you are upset by having learned too soon and too quickly things which we who live about the court have long known and accepted. You don't suppose, do you, that sensible men believe all that palaver about the sun and moon? Or imagine that the Inca, whom we all know and despise, becomes divine once a year by the calendar? We know perfectly well that no religious motives inspire him during what is called the Holy Night; but we do not make a hullabaloo about it as you threaten to do, for we know that these beliefs, however groundless they may be, are useful to the State. They cause the government to be revered, and enable us to preserve order at home and empire abroad. What do you suppose would happen if the populace came to think as you do? There would be disorders in Peru; there would be insurrections abroad; and very soon the whole fabric of civilized society would be in tatters. Rash girl! You refuse to be a sacrifice to the Inca, but you have not thought that the true sacrifice is to law and order and social stability, not to a gross prince. You prate of truth, but how can truth preserve an empire? Has the Professor failed to teach you that all empires, always, have been built upon useful lies? I am afraid you are an anarchist, and if you do not recant, you can scarcely hope that the State will show you mercy."

"Father," she replied, "it is natural, I suppose, in view of our family traditions, that the Peruvian State should be a god to you. Some effort of imagination is needed to think of another order of society than that in which you have lived all your life. And, Father, I am afraid that imagination is not your strongest point. I see in my thoughts a better world than that which our race has created: a world containing more justice, more mercy, more love, and, above all, more truth.

Cataclysms and disorders there may be on the road to this better world, but even they are to be preferred to the dead rigidity of our public and private abominations."

At this her father became red with fury, and, exclaiming in a loud voice, "Impertinent child, I leave you to your fate!" he marched out into the sunshine.

The next to visit the obstinate prisoner was the Professor. He entered her cell with an air of suave and hypothetical benignity, and addressed her in tones which masked authority by their intended persuasiveness. "My poor girl," he said, "I am sorry to see you here, and I cannot but think that some part of the blame must be mine, for in the year during which you have listened to my indoctrinating lectures I ought to have succeeded in conveying to you a more just apprehension of social duty than is indicated by your present predicament. But tell me, Diotima, at what points, and for what reasons, do you dissent from the doctrines which it has fallen to my unworthy self to endeavor to instill?"

"Well," she replied, "since you ask me, I will tell you. I don't believe your facts, I don't believe your theories. I think your conception of social utility intolerably narrow and your belief in the unchangeability of dogma so wooden as to bring death to intellect and feeling alike. I think your indifference to truth revolting, and your subservience to the powers that be toadeating and contemptible. Now, having cleared the air, I am willing to hear what you have to say."

At these rude words the Professor flushed, and for a moment he was tempted to retort with mere abuse, but that would have been to betray the traditions of his order. Diotima had been blunt. She had eschewed ambiguity and vagueness in a manner which he could not too deeply deplore. She had been content to dwell in those regions of mere fact which to the initiate are but the foothills of the lofty peaks of wisdom. Restraining his annoyance with an effort, he told himself that the girl was overwrought and that the diet of bread and water might well cause bad temper. The habits of a lifetime of lecturing came to his aid, and he replied to her diatribe in a manner truly admirable in view of his greatness and her youth.

"Diotima," he said, "there are some things that you do not seem to know and that, even at this late hour, I must put before you with all the power at my command. I will begin with what is at the basis of all else: Do you deny the Godhead of the Holy Zahatopolk?"

"I do," she replied. "We are taught that he descended from Heaven in a miraculous manner. For my part I believe that he descended in a helicopter from a plane hidden above the clouds. We are told that he did not die, but ascended miraculously into Heaven when his work on earth was ended. This, also, I do not believe. I believe that a camarilla of his generals surrounded him during his last illness and kept him from all contact with the outer world. I believe that they threw his corpse into the crater of Cotopaxi. Legends to this effect have been handed down secretly in my family, whose ancestor was the ringleader in this proceeding. All are sworn to secrecy and only the men are initiated. But men have fevers, and fevers bring delirium, and in delirium even the gravest secrets can be blabbed."

At this point the professor saw that a lecture on truth was called for. "Granted, my dear girl," he said, "that on the mundane level of sensible fact things were as you say, do you not realize that there is a higher sense in which the orthodox doctrine of our land conveys a truth more profound than any mere legend of helicopters and military camarillas? What have helicopters to do with divinity? They are mere contrivances: ingenious, no doubt; convenient, no doubt; but unworthy to hold a central place in the fundamental doctrines of cosmogony. If, indeed, our Divine Founder deigned to make use of some such mechanism, He did so, no doubt, for a wise purpose which it is not for us to question. And when you deny that He descended from Heaven, are you so certain that you know where Heaven is? Have you never learned the great spiritual truth that Heaven is wherever there are heavenly thoughts? And wherever Zahatopolk may have been, there, rest assured, heavenly thoughts had a home. Of His death very similar things may be said. What if His earthly integument became cold and lifeless? What if His disciples reverently restored it to that terrestrial fire which of all things on this earth is nearest to the Divine Fire that had enabled Him to instruct His disciples? It was not the earthly integument that was to be worshiped, for our God is to be worshiped in spirit and in truth, and spirit and truth dwell in the soul, not in the body. The rash words that you uttered concerning the Most High God may have been in some gross sense not out of harmony with material fact, but spiritually, as I have shown you, and in the only sense that concerns us as beings partaking, however imperfectly, of the Divine Essence, they are utterly false and to be condemned with all the force that our holy religion can inspire."

"Professor," the girl replied, "what you say is of course very impressive, but I have arrived at a view which I fear you may find shocking. I think that there are facts and fictions, there is truth and there are lies. I know that those who

preach the doctrine of the golden mean, of which I suspect
you of being an adherent, consider that one should observe
the golden mean between truth and falsehood, as you so ad-
mirably did in the speech to which I have just listened. But, to
my mind, facts are harsh and will not be denied. I know that
in a brutal orgy the sadistic Inca first enjoyed, and then ate,
my friend Freia. This is fact. And however you may clothe
the fact in a mantle of mist and myth, it will remain a fact,
and so long as you try to hide it from your gaze you will share
its vileness and it will pollute you."

"Come, come," said the Professor, "this is strong language,
and I cannot think that you have studied the philosophical
theory of truth as deeply as your academic duty demanded
that you should. Do you not know that the truth of a doctrine
lies in its social utility and its spiritual depth, not in some
wretched vulgar accuracy such as can be measured by a foot-
rule in the hands of a clod? Measured by any true standard,
how paltry are your feelings concerning your friend Freia!
How much more profound, how much more consonant with
the needs of the human race, was her ecstasy in those moments
of apotheosis! Consider what, for her, has been achieved.
Through a few brief moments, some aspects of which you, in
your arrogance, find revolting, she has become one with the
Moon Goddess. In eternal calm and eternal beauty, what was
imperishable in her sails through the skies, exempt from the
sorrows and tribulations of this mortal life. And consider
what mankind owes to that majestic ritual in which her earthly
life was ended. Consider the poetry, the slow-moving music,
the glorious mosaics, and the Temple whose sublime and se-
vere lines draw eye and soul alike toward heaven. Would you
have all this perish from the earth? Would you have mankind

reduced to a dusty, bookkeeping pedestrianism? Would you have poetry and music and architecture perish? Yet how could any of these survive without the divine myth (I use the words in no derogatory sense) by which they have been inspired?

"But if art and beauty mean nothing to you, what of the social structure? What of law, what of morality, what of government? Do you suppose that these could survive? Do you suppose that men would abstain from murder, and theft, and even intercourse with non-Peruvians, if they did not feel the eye of Zahatopolk upon them? And do you not see that, since the true is what is socially useful, the doctrines of our holy religion are true? Renounce, I beseech you, your self-willed pride; submit yourself to the wisdom of the ages; and, by so doing, put an end to the torment and shame that you are inflicting upon your parents, your teachers and your friends."

"No!" exclaimed Diotima. "No! A thousand times no! This higher truth of which you speak is to me only higher humbug. This social utility of which you make so much is only the preservation of unjust privilege. This marvelous morality of which you prate justifies the oppression and degradation of the great majority of the human race. My eyes are opened, and not all your tortuous words can induce me to close them again."

The Professor, incensed at last, exclaimed: "Then perish in your stiff-necked arrogance, wretched apostate! I leave you to the fate that you have so richly deserved." And with that he left her.

Only one possibility of bringing Diotima to repentance remained. It was known that Thomas had loved her, and it was hoped that she had loved Thomas. Perhaps love would effect what authority had failed to do. It was decided that Thomas should have an interview with her, but that, if he failed, no further effort should be made to turn her from the error of her ways.

Thomas had been passing through a very difficult time of conflict, fear, and misery. As a man in love, he suffered from the death of his hopes. As an ambitious youth, whose path to success hitherto had seemed plain, he dreaded the suspicion that might attach to him as the intimate friend of a heretic. As a student of theology and history, who had never on his own account seen reason to question his father's wisdom, he was appalled by the dangerous consequences that would ensue if Diotima's beliefs became common. Since her apostasy he had found many former friends avoiding him, and he saw that he was losing the position of a leader in his own group. His father, returning furious from his interview with Diotima, spoke to him with grave severity:

"Thomas," he said, "Diotima is inspired by the Spirit of Evil, to which in my theology I have hitherto given insufficient attention. Dangerous thoughts emanate from her like lurid flames from a sulphurous fire. I do not know what lodgment the poison may have found in your own brain. For your sake, I hope not much. But if you are to recover the general respect which has hitherto rejoiced my parental heart, you will have to be very clear, and make it very clear to all and sundry, that you are utterly opposed to her vile heresies, and that no lingering affection will blunt the edge of your desire to see her suffer the just penalty of her infamy. There is, however, still a faint hope. It may be that you will succeed where her parents and I have failed. If you do, all will be well. But if you do not, it will be your duty to prove by your zeal that you have suffered no contamination."

With these alarming words still ringing in his ears, Thomas

found himself admitted to Diotima's cell. For a moment the spectacle of her beauty and her calm overwhelmed him. Human love, and a passionate longing that she might yet be saved, swept away in that first instant both prudence and orthodoxy. He burst into tears and exclaimed, "Oh, Diotima, would that I could save you!"

"My poor Thomas," she replied, "how can you cherish so foolish a hope? Whatever I may do, my life is forfeit. Either I die as the Bride of Zahatopolk, with public honor and inward shame, or I die as a criminal, despised and execrated except by my own conscience."

"Your own conscience!" he answered. "How can you set it up as the sole arbiter against so much wisdom and such long ages? Oh, Diotima, how can you be so sure? How can you know that all of us are wrong? Have you no respect for my father? Are you willing to besmirch your ancestors? I have loved you. I have hoped that you might love me. But that hope, I see, was vain. It is anguish to say so, but I cannot continue to love you while you lacerate all my deepest feelings. Oh, Diotima, it is more than I can bear!"

"I am truly sorry," she said, "to have brought upon you this cruel dilemma. Hitherto, you have had every reason to expect a career both smooth and honorable. Henceforth, you have to choose. If you condemn me, your career may still be smooth. If you do not, it may be honorable. But I know, however you may disguise it from yourself, that in your heart of hearts you cannot be happy if you condemn me. You may, perhaps, during the busy hours of the day, silence your doubts while you listen to public applause; but in the night, you will see a vision in which I shall be beckoning you toward a happier world. And as you turn your back upon me, you will wake in agony. For I know that you have seen, if only briefly, that vision for the sake of which I am willing to be condemned. It is not, as we pretend, the sun and moon that inspire our official creed. It is pride and fear: pride in our Empire, and fear lest we may lose it. It is not upon these passions that human life should be built. It should be built upon truth and love. It should be lived without fear, in a happiness that all can share. It should be unable to find a contentment resting upon the degradation of others. It should be ashamed to aim at a paltry physical safety at the expense of the inner springs of joy and life which well up in those who open their spirit to the world in fearless adventure. We have let ourselves be bound in chains. Outside our own land the chains have been forced upon their victims by us. We have not realized that whoever imprisons another becomes himself a prisoner, a prisoner of fear and hate. And the chains which we have forged for others have bound us in a mental dungeon. Remember the sun that found its way into our valley. Even so, light must fall upon dark places of the world. And however little you may know it now, it will be your mission when I am dead to carry on this work."

For a moment her words found an echo in his heart. But he summoned up his resolution, and his momentary yielding turned to anger. "How can you think so! How can you think that such high-flown verbiage can make me abandon all that I revere! Further speech with you is useless. You must die. And I must live, to combat the evil that you think good." With these words he rushed from her cell.

After Thomas' failure, the authorities gave up hope of inducing Diotima to recant. A new Bride was chosen and Diotima was condemned to die publicly at the very moment when she should have enjoyed mystic unity with the Divinity.

The day of expiation was proclaimed a public holiday. The stake was erected in the central square of the city. Seats for the notables were in the front ranks. Behind, the whole population of the city stood in greedy expectation. They laughed and joked and jeered. They ate nuts and oranges. They made coarse jests, and exulted in the expectation of the torture they were about to witness. The notables in the front rows were more dignified, and the Inca on His throne was majestically silent. Thomas, as his father's son, was privileged to sit among the notables. He had been suspected of sharing Diotima's heresy, and had cleared himself of this suspicion with some vehemence. Both as a reward and as a test, he was to have a full view of her death.

She was led in naked, and preserved a calm and unmoved demeanor. The crowd shouted: "There's a wicked woman! Now she'll find out who's God!" She was tied to the stake, and flaming torches kindled the fire. As the flames reached her, she looked at Thomas—a strange and piercing look, expressing at once anguish, pity, and appeal, pity for his weakness, and appeal to carry on her work. Her anguish tore his heart, her pity bruised his manhood, and her appeal kindled in his mind a flame scarcely less searing than that which was consuming her body. In a blinding moment he saw that he had been wrong; he saw that what was being done was an abomination; he saw that she stood for what can be splendid in human life, and that the dignitaries and the multitude alike were groveling victims of bestial fear. In this one terrible moment he repented—but repentance is too mild a word for what he experienced. He experienced a passion as intense as that which

had upheld her in the flames, a passion to devote himself to the work which she could no longer perform, a passion to liberate mankind from the shackles of fear and the cruelty that it generates. He thought that he cried aloud, "Diotima, I am yours!" But in this moment he fell unconscious, and the cry must have been only in his own heart.

CHAPTER VI

Thomas

For a long time Thomas lay in hospital, gravely ill and incapable of coherent thought. Intolerable loathsome visions floated through his mind of tortured women and brutal men, of flames and death and bestial cries of triumph. Slowly, reason reasserted itself. Health returned and, with health, an inflexible determination by which his whole character was transformed. No longer was he a gentle and trusting youth willing to tread in his father's footsteps and win such easy low-level success as his father's example would secure him. With an insight born of devouring passion he saw through all the pretenses of the Peruvian system and perceived the far from laudable motives by which it was inspired and supported. His intellect, which had been trained to work with mechanical perfection within the limits imposed by orthodoxy, passed beyond those limits without losing the keen edge of pitiless accuracy. But it was not only his intellect that was liberated; it was also, and even more, his heart. Peruvians had been taught to reverence the State as the earthly garment of God, and to limit their sympathies to those who served the State to the best of their abilities. But the State had destroyed Diotima and, in rebellion against that cruelty, he found himself rebelling against all the other cruelties, all the other inhumanities, all the other institutions which fettered human sympathy, not only in his own country but wherever human beings were to be found. Love, hate, and intellect were welded together by the fire of his passion into a single steely whole; love first for Diotima, and thence, by transference, to all other victims; hate for those who condemned her, and thence for the whole system which had made this condemnation possible; intellect, which told him that the divinity of Zahatopolk was a myth, that the sun and moon were not divinities but lifeless masses, that the condemnation of birth control was superstitious, and that, in eating their children, men killed in themselves their own capacity for sympathy and kindliness. With all his mind and heart and will he resolved that, if it were in any way possible, he would establish upon earth a better system than that which he had been taught to revere, a system more in harmony with Diotima's vision. The sense of guilt which gnawed at his inmost being could, he thought, be appeased only if he could make this offering to the torturing memory of Diotima.

But the offering to her memory, if it was to appease his remorse, must be a change in the world, not a mere personal dedication or a futile martydom. With a determination inwardly white-hot, but outwardly as cold as ice, he set to work, first to think out a plan, and then to carry it into execution. In public and with all whom he could not fully trust, he breathed no word of criticism of the established order. To his father, as to almost everybody else, he appeared cleansed of whatever doubts he might once have felt. The distrust with which he had been viewed during the last days of Diotima soon passed away, and his official career marched smoothly from success to success. He acquired a position of leadership among his contemporaries, and his words were listened to as having weight and wisdom.

His most ardent friend and admirer was a young man named Paul. To Paul, at a very late hour on a summer night, he opened his heart—tentatively at first, but gradually, as he met with response, more and more completely. Paul had had misgivings about the burning of Diotima, but had wisely kept his misgivings to himself. As Thomas spoke, Paul's misgivings acquired new force. They talked through the whole summer night until the dawn appeared. They parted sworn confederates in the promotion of whatever revolution might prove possible. Gradually they gathered about them a secret society of intending rebels. Students of science found it impossible to accept the divinity of the sun and moon; students of history could not believe in the inferiority of other races; students of psychology were revolted by the cannibalistic thwarting of parental affection. Stories of the Inca's far from divine behavior filtered through from court circles in spite of all precautions. But still Thomas held his hand.

In secret he encouraged the ablest among his disciples to make researches of a kind which the government had forbidden on pain of death. Peruvian power had rested upon the death-dealing fungus of Cotopaxi, but a brilliant young physician discovered a prophylactic against the plague. Several among Thomas' confederates became governors of remote provinces, for such posts, since they involved exile from Peru, were considered disagreeable and usually given to young men as the first step in the official hierarchy. Very cautiously and very secretly, these men set to work to undo the degradation which it had been the policy of Peru to produce in other parts of the world. Paul, who remained his second-in-command, became governor of the Province of Kilimanjaro. The mountaineers of that region, owing to the austerities imposed by nature, had remained hardy and vigorous. He took their head men into his confidence and gave them, for the first time in many centuries, the hope of escape from unworthy subjection. Many of the conspirators remained in key positions in Peru, completely unsuspected by their superiors.

At length, after twenty years of careful preparation, Thomas judged that the time had come for open action. The whole course that events were to take was carefully mapped. Thomas, by this time rector of the University, announced that on a given day he would make a sensational revelation. All of his adherents, except such as had special duties assigned to them, were told to be present in the hall in which he would speak. Like his father at an earlier time, he mounted the rostrum, but the words which he spoke were very different from his father's. He avowed all his beliefs and all his disbeliefs. To the amazement of those who were not in the plot, his most subversive sentiments received loud applause. There was bewilderment and panic. But the authorities, as had been foreseen, succeeded in seizing him, and he was condemned, like Diotima, to perish in the flames on the feast of Epiphany.

What happened after this was not what the government had intended. One of his scientific friends had discovered how to make rain, and a deluge made it impossible to light the flames in which he should have perished. His friend Paul, knowing the exact hour at which the execution was to take place, dispatched from the headquarters of the government at Kilimanjaro an enormous plane which traveled at supersonic speed until it reached the rain clouds over Cuzco. From that point it dispatched a helicopter, which descended upon the marketplace and snatched up Thomas, who was borne off to Kilimanjaro leaving the populace with the unshakable conviction that they had witnessed a miracle. The government found itself paralyzed by the unsuspected disaffection of many of its officers. When the authorities of Cuzco heard of rebellion in Kilimanjaro they supposed that they could deal with it by means of the fungus plague. When they learned that the inhabitants of Africa were immune to this plague, they were seized with terror, which turned to consternation when they found that Thomas' scientists had discovered how to produce radioactive death from the volcanic slopes of the new Sacred Mountain. They had for so many centuries had no occasion for fear that in the crisis their courage failed them, and when Thomas' emissaries, in a great fleet of planes, circled above them, threatening to let loose the death-dealing dust that they had brought with them, the whole governing aristocracy surrendered on the promise that their lives should be spared. Kilimanjaro became the center of government. Thomas was proclaimed the President of the World, and Paul was appointed his prime minister. All recognized that a new era had begun and that the age of Zahatopolk was ended.

Thomas, as soon as his regime was secure, set to work to undo the degradation to which non-Indian populations had been subjected. He diminished the hours of physical work, which the Peruvians had kept to ten, not from any economic motive, but only in order that the workers might be too tired to have any initiative. By means of his faithful band of scientists, he greatly increased the world's food supply, and by declaring the preventing of conception innocent, made the increase minister to health and happiness, and not only to more rapid multiplication. He gave a share of political power to all who had sufficient education, and he extended education as quickly as possible throughout all parts of the world. In many of the hitherto oppressed countries there was a great outburst of painting and poetry and music. The suppressed energies, which had lain dormant for centuries, sprang into a luxuriant life such as had only been known before in a few countries in a few great ages. He taught that there are no gods. And, although the populace ascribed his escape to a miracle, he did his best to persuade the world that miracles are impossible. There were those who wished to give him the position that Zahatopolk had previously had, but he refused deification with emphasis and caused the doctrine to be combated in all the schools. Under his regime there were no priests and no aristocrats, no ruling races and no subject peoples.

CHAPTER VII

The Future

The above is the account of the Great Revolution given by Thomas' friend Paul after Thomas' reign of many years had been brought to an end by his death. This account of his life and doctrines has remained ever since the Sacred Book of the Kilimanjaro Era. But it has gradually been found that some parts of Thomas' doctrine are liable to misinterpretation, and that the reading of Paul's book by all and sundry may be dangerous. He was not always careful to indicate when he was to be taken literally and when he was speaking allegorically. It is now universally recognized that Thomas was in fact a god, and that Diotima was a goddess. We know that both for a time put on humanity, but at the moment of their earthly death resumed their heavenly life, which for a few brief years they had put away for our salvation. When Thomas denied his godhead he was, as all now acknowledge, denying it only as regards his earthly manifestation. All this was carefully explained about five hundred years after his death by the great commentator Gregorius.

For a time Paul's book was still allowed to circulate, provided the commentary of Gregorius was bound up with it. But even this was found to have dangers, and the book, even with the commentary, is now not allowed to be read except by licensed divines. Even so, it remains a danger. New Zealand contains one copy in the University of Auckland. This copy was lately returned to the University with a strange note upon its last page. The note said:

"I, Tupia, of the tribe of Ngapuhi, a dweller upon the slopes of Ruapehu, am not persuaded of the justice of Gregorius' glosses. I am convinced that Thomas was wiser than Gregorius, and that he meant literally all the things which that theologically minded priest finds troublesome. It shall be my mission, if possible, to lead the world back to that ancient unfaith which its liberator tried to spread."

These are ominous words, and their outcome is as yet uncertain.

Faith and Mountains

CHAPTER I

The Nepalese delegate to UNESCO was surprised and puzzled. It was the first time that he had abandoned the safety of his native glaciers and precipices for the bewildering perils of the West. Arriving by air late on the previous evening, he had been too tired to notice anything, and had slept heavily until the morning was well advanced. He looked out upon a street which, as he was informed by the waiter who brought his breakfast, was called Piccadilly. But it did not wear the aspect which the cinema had led him to anticipate. There was no ordinary traffic, but an immense procession of men and women on foot bearing banners of which his phrasebook did not enable him to guess the meaning. The inscriptions on the banners were repeated at such frequent intervals that at last he had deciphered them all. They said various things which, he was compelled to suppose, all pointed one moral. The commonest was "Hail to Molybdenum, Maker of Healthy Bodies!" Another which occurred with great frequency was "Up with the Molybdenes!" A third, not quite so frequent, said, "Long Life to the Holy Molly B. Dean!" One peculiarly ferocious band had a banner saying, "Death to the Infamous Magnets!" The procession was of enormous length and, at intervals of about a quarter of a mile, there was a band and a choir which sang what appeared to be the battle hymn of the marchers:

> Molybdenum of metals best
> Is good for high and low.
> It cures diseases of the chest
> And makes our muscles grow.

This hymn was sung to the tune of "There is a book who runs may read," but this the delegate did not know, as he had not had the benefit of a Christian upbringing.

After he had begun to think that the procession would never end, there came a gap. Then a solid squadron of mounted police. And then another procession, with quite other banners. Some of these said, "Glory to Aurora Bohra!" Others said, "All Power to the Northern Pole!" Yet others said, "Through Magnetism to Magnificence!" The marchers in this second procession also sang a hymn, as unintelligible to him as the hymn of the first procession. They sang:

> I go forth
> To the North
> In my jet-propelled chariot.

I descend on the Pole
For the good of my soul
And learn to think Bohra much better than Harriet.

With every moment his curiosity increased. At last it became overwhelming. He rushed out into the street and joined the procession. With true oriental courtesy he addressed his neighbor pedestrian with the words: "Would you, sir, deign to have the great kindness to explain to me why this musical multitude marches westward with such rhythmic persistence?"

"Lor bless yer!" said the man he addressed. "Mean to say yer don't know about the Magnets? And where may you have come from?"

"Sir," replied the delegate, "you must bear with my ignorance. I have but recently dropped from the skies, and have dwelt hitherto in the Himalayas, in a region inhabited only by Buddhists and Communists, who are quiet, peaceable folk, not addicted to such singular pilgrimages."

"Gorblimey!" said his neighbor. "If that's so, it would take more breath than I can spare to make you understand!"

The delegate therefore marched on in silence, hoping that time would bring enlightenment.

At length the procession arrived at an enormous round building which, as his neighbor informed him, was called the Albert Hall. Some of the procession were admitted within, but the great majority were compelled to remain without. The Nepalese at first was refused admission. But, on explaining his official position as a delegate, and the profound interest of his country in Occidental cultural phenomena, he was at last allowed to take a seat far back in the exact middle of the platform.

What he saw and what he heard seemed to him to throw a great light upon the manners and customs, the beliefs and habits of thought of the strange people among whom he found himself. But so much remained unintelligible to him that he determined to devote himself to serious research and to draw up an elucidatory report for the enlightment of Himalayan sages.

The work proved onerous, and it was not until twelve months had passed that he deemed it worthy of the wise eyes of those who had sent him. During these twelve months I had had the good fortune to make friends with him, and to be allowed to share in his wisdom. The following account of the great debate, and the events that led up to it and followed it, is based upon his report. Without his labors, my account could not have been so exhaustive or so minutely accurate.

CHAPTER II

The two sects, whose public debate the Nepalese delegate witnessed, had each emerged after a period of obscurity, and had, in recent years, grown with such amazing rapidity that hardly anybody, except highbrows, failed to belong to one or other. They were called, respectively, the Molybdenes and the Northern Magnets, or simply the Magnets. Each had its head office in London. The affairs of the Molybdenes were directed by Zeruiah Tomkins, and those of the Magnets by Manasseh Merrow. In each case the fundamental doctrine of the sect was simple.

The Molybdenes believed that the human frame requires,

for full development of health and strength, a larger amount of molybdenum in the diet than has hitherto been customary. Their favorite text was: "He that eateth, eateth unto the Lord. And he that eateth not, unto the Lord he eateth not." But they changed the order of the words in the latter half of this text so as to make it read: "He that eateth not, eateth not unto the Lord." He that eateth, they explained, means a person who eats molybdenum. They supported their position by a story for whose truth I cannot vouch. Large flocks of sheep in a certain district of Australia, which had withered away, had slowly perished because their scanty pastures, unlike those of Europe and Asia, were wholly destitute of molybdenum. Certain biochemists and medical men—not perhaps quite the most eminent in their respective professions—had made statements as to the dietetic importance of molybdenum, and these statements were seized upon by the faithful as supports for their creed. There had been a considerable demand for this not very common metal in armaments, but the gradual lessening of tension had diminished this demand. Now, however, owing to the growth of the Molybdenes, the demand for molybdenum had ceased to be dependent upon the threat of war. The Molybdenes were opposed to war. They regarded all men as brothers, except the Northern Magnets; and the Northern Magnets were to be overcome, not by force of arms, but by the pure light of truth.

The Northern Magnets found the secret of human welfare in a quite different direction, "We are all," so they said, "the children of Earth, and the Earth, as every schoolboy knows, is a great magnet. We must all share, in a greater or less degree, the magnetic propensities of our Mighty Mother, but, if we do not submit ourselves to her beneficent authority, we shall become unclear and confused. We should therefore always sleep with our heads toward the North Magnetic Pole and our feet toward the South Magnetic Pole. Those who persistently sleep thus will gradually acquire a share in the magnetic powers of Earth. They will be healthy, vigorous, and wise." So at least the Northern Magnets unshakably believed.

In both sects there was an inner and an outer circle. The inner circle were called "Adepts"; and the outer circle, "Adherents." Inner and outer circle alike had a badge by which they could be known. The Molybdenes wore a ring made of molybdenum, and the Northern Magnets wore a magnet as a locket. The Adepts devoted themselves to the holy life, consisting partly in observances and partly in missionary work. Both communities of Adepts were healthy, happy, and virtuous. Alcohol and tobacco were forbidden them. They went early to bed, the Molybdenes in order that the health-giving molybdenum they had consumed might be absorbed into the blood stream, the Northern Magnets in order that the magnetic powers of Earth might operate fully during the hours of darkness. Sustained by faith, the Adepts were little troubled by the daily rubs which ruffle the tempers of those not sustained in this way. True, they had in early days had their difficulties. Unwise zealots had pushed the eminently sane doctrines of the two sects beyond the limits of wisdom. At one time there was among the Molybdenes an extreme faction which thought that holiness could be measured by the amount of molybdenum consumed each day. Some went so far that their skin became metallic, and it was found that, sublime as were their intentions, in molybdenum, as in everything else, it was possible to indulge to excess. The elders, after a stormy meeting, were compelled to discipline the zealots. But after this painful incident no similar trouble again arose.

Among the Magnets there was a different deviation into fanaticism. There were those who said: "If virtue comes while we lie prone in the direction of the lines of terrestrial magnetic force, it is clear that we ought always to lie thus, and that to rise from our beds is to risk dissipation of the vivificatory virtue that Earth confers upon those who duly worship her." These zealots accordingly spent the whole twenty-four hours in bed, to the no small inconvenience of their less ardent relatives and friends. This heresy, like that of the Molybdenes, was subdued, though with difficulty, by the authority of the elders, and it was decreed that, except in times of ill-health, no Northern Magnet should spend more than twelve hours out of twenty-four in his bed.

Both these troubles, however, belonged to the early days of the two sects. In their later days, missionary ardor and swift success combined with health and vigor to fill their lives with joy. One thing only troubled the Adepts: The Molybdenes could not understand why Providence permitted the growth of the Northern Magnets; and the Northern Magnets could not understand why Providence permitted the growth of the Molybdenes. Each sect consoled itself with the thought that there must be mystery somewhere, and that it is not given to the finite intellect of man to fathom the august designs of Providence. Doubtless, in the fullness of time, truth would prevail, and the sect which had throughout proclaimed the truth would win universal adherence. Meantime, it was the duty of the Adepts, by example, by precept, by wise words in and out of season, to spread the light. In this effort, the success of both parties was, to the indifferent, amazing.

In early days, each sect had had to face the ridicule of unbelievers. "Why molybdenum?" said these scoffers. "Why not strontium? What not barium? What is the peculiar glory of this one element?" When the believers replied that this was a mystery intelligible only to those who already had faith, the answer was received with derision.

The Northern Magnets had equal difficulties to face. "Why not the South Magnetic Pole?" said the skeptics. Some, especially certain inhabitants of the Southern hemisphere, went so far as to sleep habitually with their heads toward the South, and challenged Northern Magnets to wrestling matches designed to prove that the South Magnetic Pole is as invigorating as the one in the North. Such challenges were treated by the Northern Magnets with the contempt that they deserved. They replied that, while those who followed the prescribed regimen would achieve physical health and strength, it was not this alone that they would achieve, but an inner harmony through interpenetration by the magnetic might of Earth. In mere brawn some among them might be surpassed by some among unbelievers. In the perfect harmony of body and spirit true believers would remain supreme. And as for the pretense that the South Pole was just as good as the North Pole, how, if this were true, could it be explained why the Creator had made so much more land in the North than in the South? This argument, though it aroused some anger in South America, South Africa, and Australia, was felt to be very difficult to meet. Only the firm fervor of the Molybdenes was impervious to the arguments of the Northern Magnets.

Each side urged, and urged with justice, that to meet faith in falsehood, only faith in truth was adequate. Never could cold reason unaided prevail against the misleading ardor of deluded fanatics. While the two sects were still young, some men of science and some literary satirists had endeavored to meet their claims by the combined force of statistics and ridicule. But they had been powerless to stem the popular tide, and, in time, only men whom superior intelligence (or what they themselves deemed such) had cut off from sympathy with the mass of mankind stood out against both sects. The more expensive newspapers, which had small circulations, and were read only by the aristocracy of intellect, continued to remain aloof and neutral. They said as little as they could about the doings of the two sects, with the result that persons of superior education were almost unaware of what was happening round about them. The cheaper newspapers tried at first to placate both parties, but this proved impossible. Any word of praise of the Northern Magnets roused all Molybdenes to fury. Any not derogatory mention of the Molybdenes caused the Northern Magnets to vow that they would never again read so degraded a journal. The popular newspapers were therefore compelled to take sides. The *Daily Lightning* sided with the Northern Magnets; the *Daily Thunder* with the Molybdenes. Day by day, each portrayed more luridly than before the moral and intellectual degradation of the opposite party and the almost incredible heights of purity, devotion and vigor achieved by the party which the journal supported. Under the influence of such journalistic skill party spirit ran higher and higher, national unity was lost, and it was even feared that civil war might ensue.

Nor was the trouble confined to Britain. Indeed its gravest aspect was an increasing tension between the United States and Canada, which came about through causes that we have not yet set forth.

CHAPTER III

The founder of the Molybdenes was a certain middle-aged American widow named Molly B. Dean. Her husband had been a very rich man, but meek with that kind of meekness which, according to the Gospels, inherits the earth. He possessed, partly by inheritance and partly by skillful investment, a great deal of the earth of Colorado. His wife, to whom he left the whole of his immense fortune, was one of those ladies who are obviously born to be widows. Those who marry such ladies never achieve old age. And Mr. Dean duly died in the prime of life. She, however, appears not to have recognized this as an inevitable part of her destiny, for, when discoursing on the merits of molybdenum, she was wont to say: "Ah, had I but known of the beneficent effects of this metal sooner, my dear husband Jehoshaphat might still be on this side of the Great Veil!"

Mrs. Molly B. Dean, whose religion and business acumen were perhaps not quite so separate as one could wish, discovered, on examining her husband's investments after his death, that she owned about nine-tenths of the world's supply of molybdenum ore. She was struck by the similarity between the name of this element and her own name. Such similarity, she felt convinced, could not be due to chance. It must be the work of Destiny. It must be her glorious mission to give her name to a new faith, purer than any previous faith and not less profitable to herself.

The adherents of the new faith should be taught to consume molybdenum, and should be named, after herself, the Molybdenes. The offspring of the moment of creative thought grew rapidly and was soon able to walk upon its two legs of religious faith and business acumen. Lest either should interfere with the other, she formed a company, called Amalgamated Metals Inc., of which she retained control, although her name did not appear. At the same time, she poured her religious beliefs into the mind of Zeruiah Tomkins, a man somewhat younger than herself, who had had great success as a Baptist preacher, but had fallen into disfavor through a slight lapse from orthodoxy. Her powerful personality dominated him completely. He accepted her every word as divine revelation, and became filled with an immense ardor for the regeneration of mankind through her very original gospel. His organizing capacity was as great as his zeal; and she entrusted to him, without a qualm, the terrestrial affairs of the holy brotherhood of the Molybdenes.

The Northern Magnets owed their origin, though they themselves were unaware of this fact, to an important man named Sir Magnus North. Sir Magnus was a prominent figure in the national life of Canada and the owner of vast tracts of land in the empty Northwest, which he believed to be possessed of great mineral wealth. He decided to put the Northwest "on the map." He employed eminent geophysicists to locate the Magnetic Pole more accurately than had hitherto been done, and discovered, as he had hoped, that it was in the very middle of the lands of which he was owner. He discovered also, or rather the explorers whom he employed discovered, that at the Magnetic Pole there is a volcanic mountain, and, whether from volcanic action or as a result of radioactivity, the soil in the neighborhood is warm, snow does not lie, and there is a lake which even in winter remains unfrozen. With these data in his possession he planned a great campaign. With the

help of a professor of anthropology who had studied the beliefs of Eskimos and Northern Indians, he formulated the
main tenets of the creed which became that of the Northern
Magnets. But, as he was warned by the anthropologist, and as
he knew from experiences on the Stock Exchange, it is not by
pure reason that men are governed. Although to a rational
mind the arguments in favor of the creed which he wished to
propagate must prove irresistible, he sought and found a key
to men's hearts at once softer and more compelling. He realized that it was not for him to be the missionary of the new
sect. The missionary must be at once dynamic and mystical,
someone capable of appealing to the deepest chords of the
human heart, someone who could introduce into the feelings
of men and women that strange unquiet peace which seems to
bring happiness, but does not bring slothful inactivity.

The search for such a founder he left in the hands of his
anthropologist, who interviewed the leaders of sects in Los
Angeles, in Chicago, and wherever new beliefs were being
ardently sought. Acting on the orders of Sir Magnus, he did
not reveal his purpose. At last he prepared a short list of
three, and submitted it to Sir Magnus for his final decision.
Of the three, there was one whom Sir Magnus judged to be
outstanding. She had been electrifying Winnipeg, of which
she was a native, by the promise of a great revelation to come;
but what the nature of the revelation should be she had not yet
told. She was a lady of majestic proportions: her height was
six foot four, and all her other dimensions were to scale. Many
of those who beheld her were reminded of the Statue of Liberty, but she was even more august. There was only one thing
against her, and that was her name, which was Amelia Skeggs.
Sir Magnus, when he reflected upon the future for which he

hoped, found it difficult to imagine the world adhering to Skeggendom or Skeggianity. He remembered the fate of the Muggletonians, who had everything in their favor, except the unfortunate name Muggleton. For a time this difficulty made him hesitate, but in the end he found a triumphant solution. When he had found it, he decided that the time had come to reveal to the majestic Amelia the great destiny which he planned for her.

"Miss Skeggs," he said, "I know from your eloquent preaching that you are aware of a great destiny. Nature has fashioned you to dominate mankind not only by your splendid frame but by the greatness of the soul that inhabits it. You know that you are to have a mission; but you have not known until now what that mission is to be. It is left to me, as the humble emissary of Providence, to show you the way to that towering spiritual eminence for which you know yourself to be destined." He then explained to her the tenets which became those of the Northern Magnets.

As he spoke, she became filled with spiritual fire. Not a doubt remained anywhere. This was the gospel which she had been seeking. This was the happy truth which should make Canada the Holy Land, and lead the faithful of all the world, in humble pilgrimages, to its magnetic shrine.

One step remained for Sir Magnus. "You must have in religion," he said, "a different name from that which you have had in the world; a dedicated name, a name whose very syllables reverberate your sacred task. Henceforth, you shall be known to all the nations of the world by a new and splendid appellation: All Hail to You,

AURORA BOHRA!"

She left his presence intoxicated, exalted, filled with mystic ecstacy and high purpose. From that moment, their collaboration was perfect. But, acting upon his instructions, she kept his part secret.

It did not take long for Aurora Bohra to become known and successful in wide circles. She was fortunate in obtaining the assistance of Manasseh Merrow, a man who, while possessed of great organizing ability, had always been conscious of a lack in himself, a lack of those spiritual qualities which, as a youth, he had admired in the memory of his sainted mother. This lack was made up to him by Aurora Bohra, for whom he felt a devout and unfaltering worship. If anyone had asked him whether he loved her, he would have been outraged by the blasphemy. It was not love, but adoration that he felt for her. He laid at her feet all his great ability in practical affairs, and left her free for the expression of that mellifluous ecstasy upon which her hold on men and women depended.

CHAPTER IV

One of the first enterprises to which the Northern Magnets owed their success was the creation of the great circular sanatorium surrounding the Magnetic Pole. To this sanatorium was given the name of the Magnetic Home. In this enormous edifice the head of every bed pointed exactly toward the North Magnetic Pole which occupied the center of the circular courtyard. The foot of every bed pointed exactly toward the South Magnetic Pole. Owing to the situation of this sanatorium, the curative effects of terrestrial magnetism were far greater than elsewhere. Most of the Adherents secured both mental and physical health by obeying the ordinary regimen;

but there were some who, in the early months of their disciple-ship, retained traces of a neurasthenia which they had brought from their days of unbelief. Such unquiet spirits, provided they had the necessary means, were transported in luxurious jet planes to the Polar sanatorium where every luxury was provided, and where alcohol and tobacco, elsewhere forbid-den to the faithful, were permitted for medicinal purposes.

One of the earliest of these neurasthenic visitors to the sana-torium, whose name was Jedidiah Jelliffe, had been driven to the verge of insanity by hopeless love for an exquisitely beau-tiful lady named Harriet Hemlock. The magnetism of Aurora Bohra completely cured him. And, in gratitude for his cure, he celebrated his liberation in immortal verse, which became the marching hymn of the Northern Magnets and which had bewildered the ears of the Nepalese delegate.

At the exact location of the Magnetic Pole, which was in the precise center of the circular courtyard, there was a flag staff from which floated at most times the banner of the North-ern Magnets, which represented the head of Aurora Bohra with the Aurora Borealis streaming from it in all directions. But once every day, after a period during which the faithful, under the threat of dire penalties, were compelled to avert their gaze, the flag was replaced by an eyrie from which, dressed in flowing back robes, the majestic priestess spoke her words of inspired wisdom. Above her head were nine loud-speakers, eight of them horizontal, pointing north, south, east, and west, northeast, southwest, southeast, and northwest. These were trumpets of silver. But there was in addition another loud-speaker, a trumpet of pure gold, pointing straight up-ward in order that her words might be heard in heaven as well as on earth.

Standing upon a pedestal unseen by the faithful below, in a slowly rotating circular chamber with walls of the most translucent glass, with arms waving as though in an incipient embrace and her whole body slowly undulating as though obeying the lines of a magnetic stream, with her great eyes piercing and yet contemplative, sometimes flashing, sometimes veiled, she spoke. Her voice, which was unlike any that the hearers had heard elsewhere, combined the majesty of rolling mountain thunder with the lingering gentleness of the dove.

"Dear Brothers and Sisters in Magnetism," she would say, "it is my privilege once again to speak to you of our Holy Faith, and to convey, by the power mysteriously vouchsafed to me, the strength and peace of our Magnetic Mother Earth. Through my veins flows Her fire; in my thoughts dwells Her ineffable calm. Both shall come, though perhaps in diminished degree, to you, My beloved Hearers. Is your life troubled and unquiet? Do you fear that the ardent affection, which you once received from your husband or your wife, is less than it was? Does your business fail to prosper? Do your neighbors treat you with less respect than, I am sure, you deserve? Be not troubled, dear Friends. The arms of our great Mother Earth enfold you. Your sorrows, permitted for a moment, are but intended to try your faith. Lay aside your burdens, and let Magnetic Health flow into you. Love, strength, and joy be yours, as they are mine!"

All who heard her were affected in their different ways. The weary became alert; the despondent were filled with peace; those who had been embittered by grievances began to feel them trivial; and, in the adoration of Aurora, all found themselves united in a mutual harmony.

The Molybdenes also had their recreative palace, situated at the top of Acme Alp in Colorado. This was a mountain some ten thousand feet high, covered in snow during eight months of the year, but, during the other four, lovely with mountain meadows carpeted with gentians and other wild flowers. From its summit there was a vast prospect in every direction of mountains and valleys, woods, and streams, and the red Colorado River winding its way through obstacles in the distance. It was not, however, the beauty of the prospect alone that recommended this site to Molly B. Dean. It had another, and perhaps even greater, merit in her eyes. Acme Alp was at the very center of the molybdenum region over which she held sway. The recreative palace at its summit was known far and wide as the Acme Sanitarium. Owing to the steepness of the hillside it could be reached only by helicopter. Visitors were brought by plane to Denver, and there transshipped into one of the great fleet of these ingenious machines kept always in readiness for the guests of that luxurious establishment.

Although perhaps less theatrical than the Magnet Sanatorium, the Acme Sanitarium was no whit less comfortable. New arrivals, it is true, were sometimes a little alarmed by the unusual quality of the menu. They would find that they were being offered for their first dinner Molydacious Mulligatawny, Molyb Polyp, Molybdenized Mutton, and Molyfluous Meringues—or some variant, for Molly B. Dean was aware that monotony was of all things to be avoided, and the Molybdenic quality of the diet therefore underwent different disguises on different evenings. There was a great difference between the atmosphere created by Molly B. Dean and that diffused by Aurora Bohra. Aurora Bohra believed in the mystic powers of Earth, and encouraged a certain passive receptivity as the source of subsequent vigorous action. Molly B. Dean, on the contrary, believed in calling out in each individual his own strength, his own power of will, his own control over his destiny. Not for her the reliance upon external help! In her stirring radio addresses, to which, before the evening meal, the guests in her sanitarium were compelled to listen, she would appeal to each man and each woman—aye, and to each child, too—to draw upon that inner fund of determination, upon which, in the last resort, we must all depend. She had worked out a technique for the development of these powers:

"Do you," she would say, "feel a reluctance to rise from your bed in the morning? Do not yield to it! Begin your waking day with a firm act of will. Mount your mechanical horse, and, after five minutes of strenuous exertion with this health-giving implement, devote yourself to muscular exercises unassisted by adjuncts. Touch your toes with your hands ninety-nine times while keeping your knees as stiff as a ramrod. After this, you will feel no hardship in your cold bath, though the water be obtained from melting snow. Your toilet completed, you will descend to your communal breakfast filled with appetite and energy, ready for whatever the day may bring. Is your mail full of tiresome chores? What of it? You dispose of it with only a tiny fragment of the power derived from your pre-breakfast regimen. Have your investments diminished in value? That need not trouble you, for the intellectual clarity derived from the mechanical horse will enable you, without difficulty, to select, with shrewd judgment, new investments of which the future prosperity is unquestionable. And should sinful thoughts come, as come they may even in this Holy Palace; should you permit yourself to wish that a longer period in bed, or a less frigid bath, were permitted; should you hanker after nonmolybdenized mutton; should you even, tempted doubtless by Satan, harbor the dreadful thought that strontium might do just as well—in all or any of these terrible situations you can find salvation by a simple rule: you must first run ten times round the courtyard of the palace, and then open at haphazard the Sacred Volume, *Molybdenum, the Cure for Morbid Mopings.* Wherever this volume may open you will find your eye resting upon some health-giving text, and you will be able, by your own strength, to banish the horrid thoughts which had been diverting the pure stream of your unsullied life-force. Above all, remember this: It is not in thought that salvation is to be found, but in action, strenuous action, health-giving action, action that generates power. When the wiles of Satan threaten to ensnare you, it is not to tortuous thought that you must turn, but to action. And what that action should be, you will find in the Sacred Volume. Action! Action! Action! Action in the Holy Name of Molybdenum!"

CHAPTER V

The business management of the two recreative palaces was left by Molly B. Dean and Aurora Bohra in the hands of their respective managers, Mr. Tomkins and Mr. Merrow. Each of these men realized that the sect of which he was in charge was exposed to the enmity of the other sect. Each was persuaded that the other sect consisted of unscrupulous scoundrels, who would shrink from nothing to effect the ruin of their rivals. Each therefore installed, not only in the public rooms, but in every bedroom, dictaphones which recorded the supposedly private conversations of the guests. Each found that there were grumblers, nay even incipient skeptics, who had somehow found admission in spite of all the care of the reception committee.

In Acme Alp the center of disaffection was traced, by skillful secret service work, to a certain Mr. Wagner. Mr. Wagner had seemed to the Management exactly the sort of man for whom the sanitarium was designed. He had been, the Management understood, a successful businessman, but had become afflicted with indecision. He would say, "I have studied the merits of this and that, and have found the arguments exactly evenly balanced. What, in these circumstances, am I to do?" There was a danger that in this mood his fortune would be dissipated. He had sought salvation with the Molybdenes, and had apparently hoped to find it. But although his condition improved, the cure remained incomplete, and it was decided that a period at Acme Alp would be necessary. With due submission to the authorities, he agreed. And, leaving his business interests for the time being in the hands of subordinates, he sought the health-giving atmosphere of that strenuous House of Rest.

But his conversation while there was of a sort that it was difficult to approve. He would say, addressing some chance acquaintance after dinner, "You know, it is marvelous what molybdenum does for the Molybdenes! But there are some things that puzzle me, and to which I find no answer in the Sacred Volume. Since molybdenum is mainly concentrated in Colorado, one must suppose that the inhabitants of this state consume more of it than those who live in other parts of this great republic. But, on examining the vital statistics, I have not discovered any measurable difference between the health of Colorado and that of other states. This, I confess, puzzles me. Another thing also gave me pause: I asked a scientific physician of my acquaintance to examine minutely the imports and exports of molybdenum in the body of a devout Molybdene, who has consumed that amount of the Sacred Metal prescribed by our revered Leader, and in an ordinary citizen. I found, to my amazement, that the amount of molybdenum retained in the body of a healthy Molybdene is no greater than that retained in the body of a man whose diet is normal. I am sure there must be an answer to these perplexities, but I wish I knew what it is. I do not wish to trouble Mr. Tomkins, who is a very busy man. Can you suggest some way of resolving my difficulties?"

It was found that he had made speeches of this sort to a number of people at Acme Alp. But nothing definite could be proved against him, and, in the end, it was decided to pronounce him cured and send him back to his home.

A somewhat similar trouble arose shortly afterward at the magnetic home. A certain Mr. Thorney, who was, or was supposed to be, a traveler in out-of-the-way lands, returned from an expedition, or so he said, worn out with the hardships that a series of mishaps had imposed upon him. Weary and discouraged, he sought the life-giving force that the Northern Magnets offered. He became an Adherent, and his friends among the faithful hoped for rapid improvement. But improvement was discouragingly slow, and he seemed incapable of feeling again the zest which had sent him upon his travels. It was decided by the authorities that only a visit to the Magnetic Pole could complete his cure. There, however, as on Acme Alp, dictaphones had been installed by the wise prudence of those who foresaw the machinations of their rivals.

And it was found that, while Mr. Thorney's conversation could not be condemned as definitely heretical, it had nevertheless a subtle tendency to diminish the firmness of belief in those who listened to it. It was suspected that he had not a due reverence for Aurora Bohra, whom the faithful never saw except when she was in her eyrie. "Have you ever wondered," he would say to a neighbor, "how tall Aurora really is?" "No," the neighbor would say in a slightly shocked tone, "and I am not sure that I consider the question quite nice." "Oh well," Mr. Thorney would reply, "she is, after all, a real woman of flesh and blood. Having had to practice surveying in my travels, I took the liberty of estimating her height with my sextant. Allowing for her feet, which I could not see, I concluded that her height is between six foot three and a half inches and six foot four and a half inches. I could not make my estimate more exact because of the refracting properties of the glass through which we see her. But I was able to assure myself beyond a doubt that she is a fine figure of a woman."

It was not the thing to speak in these terms of the presiding Goddess; but it must be acknowledged, though with pain, that there were some who fell in with Mr. Thorney's manner, and were thenceforth less inclined to attribute supernatural powers to that noble lady. Where he found favorable soil for the seeds of his irreverence, he would go farther. He would say, "You know, there is a circumstance, known perhaps to few white men except myself, which I find very difficult to explain on the basis of the magnetic principles that we all accept. There is, in a certain very remote part of Tibet, a valley of quite extraordinary narrowness, almost a chasm, which points, as my survey assured me, directly toward the North Magnetic Pole. Although the valley is so narrow, there are those who spend the summer in it, because it contains diamonds. They have to sleep with their heads toward the north or with their heads toward the south. Some choose the one, some the other. One might have expected that those who sleep with their heads toward the north would be in all respects superior to those who choose the opposite posture. But, although I spent a considerable time among them and made inquiries into their past history, I was unable to discover any such difference as our Holy Faith compels us to postulate. There is, I am sure, some quite conclusive answer, but I have been unable to imagine what it may be. If you, or any of your friends, can resolve my perplexity, you will earn my deepest gratitude."

When dictaphones revealed his habit of putting such questions to the other visitors in the circular palace, it was decided by the authorities that, though he was doubtless a genuine seeker after truth, the form and method of his search were not such as to deserve encouragement. He was therefore prematurely pronounced cured, and sent home, with a caution to meditate in silence, if at all, upon the curious questions that he had somewhat rashly raised.

CHAPTER VI

In spite of such slight difficulties, both movements prospered. The Northern Magnets won the support of everybody in Scandinavia, except the intelligentsia. Iceland and Greenland followed suit, and their men of science proved conclusively that, in course of time, the Magnetic Pole would be theirs. In the United States it was the Molybdenes who flourished. The state of Utah, where considerable stores of molybdenum were dis-

covered, solemnly abandoned the *Book of Mormon* and substituted *Molybdenum, the Cure for Morbid Mopings*. As some
reward for this accession to the True Faith, Molly B. Dean
conceded that Utah should be incorporated in the Holy Land.
Throughout the Western world, the bewildered young, who
had been unable to choose wholeheartedly either the Kremlin
or the Vatican as objects of adoration, found mental and emo-
tional rest in one or other of the two new creeds.

In England, where the two factions were very evenly balanced, acute conflict was more threatened than anywhere else.
Test matches no longer aroused interest, the older football
teams were forgotten, and only the great matches between
Molybdenes and Magnets attracted the crowds. Not only in
football, but in every kind of athletic contest, the Molybdenes
and the Magnets competed with fluctuating success and without decisive superiority for either. It was found, with some
dismay, that the crowds were no longer good-natured, and that
fights broke out between irascible adherents of the rival faiths.
At last a rule had to be adopted separating Molybdenes and
Magnets by placing one of these to the right and one to the
left. Those who avowed themselves neutrals were viewed with
contempt and told to go home.

The highbrows would have been delighted to make their
peace with both, but this was impossible. "He that is not with
us is against us," such temporizers were firmly told. Nevertheless, some attempt at conciliation persisted. The *Tempora
Supplementary Letters* had a deeply reflective article on the
two creeds. "It must be conceded," so this article said, "that
to the coldly critical intellect, there are difficulties in both the
gospels which are bringing new hopes and new life to the
weary West. But those who are imbued with the great tradi-

tion, those who have absorbed and digested the message of all the great thinkers, from Plato to St. Thomas Aquinas, will not lightly reject new faiths, even though they may appear impossible, as the Christian faith did to Tertullian, who, in spite of such impossibility—nay, because of it—accepted wholeheartedly the new tenets which transcended reason. All right-thinking people, whatever difficulty they may have in choosing between the Molybdenes and the Magnets, will welcome what the two movements have in common. Not so long ago a coldly mechanist philosophy dominated the thoughts of our accepted pundits. Those deeper sources of wisdom, which are not derived from mere observation of brute fact, but well up in the humble heart when it opens itself to the operation of the Great Spirit of Truth—from these the Molybdenes and the Magnets alike derive refreshment. Gone is the insolence of sciolists; gone is the shallow certainty of those who ignore the eternal verities upon which our Western world is founded. In the Molybdenes and the Magnets alike there is so much that every lover of wisdom must welcome, that we cannot but regret their separateness and rivalry. We believe, and in this belief we are not alone, that an amalgamation is possible, and that, if effected, it will give to the faith in our Western values that unshakable strength which is needed in the fateful contest with the atheism of the East."

This weighty pronouncement had influential backing. The British government, torn between love of the Commonwealth and dependence upon the United States, viewed with the deepest alarm the growing tension between Canada and the western half of the United States. Such tension, if it could not be eased, could bring to nought the work, not only of the United Nations, but also of NATO. In England, the adherents of the two parties were about equal in numbers. Both were strong, but neither could hope to be supreme. The British government approached Mr. Tomkins and Mr. Merrow with proposals for a conference, and with earnest suggestions for at least a *modus vivendi* between the two sects.

Mr. Tomkins and Mr. Merrow consulted by long-distance telephone the high priestesses, Molly B. Dean and Aurora Bohra. Aurora Bohra secretly consulted Sir Magnus North. The outcome of these various consultations was the decision to hold a great meeting in the Albert Hall at which, by public debate, some form of agreement was to be reached. Such at least was the outcome for which the government hoped. But the hopes of the two parties were different. Each was so firmly persuaded of its own invincibility that it felt no doubt of victory in a public confrontation, and it was in virtue of this confidence that each side assented to the government's proposals.

It was agreed that the great meeting should be held under the chairmanship of the Professor of Comparative Religion at the University of Oxbridge. This wise and urbane scholar knew all about the religion of the extinct Tasmanians, the beliefs of the Hottentots, and the creed of the Pygmies. It was therefore supposed by the government that he could give sympathetic understanding to both the Molybdenes and the Magnets. But, lest he should fail, through being more urbane than forceful, he was to be supported by a band of some hundreds of stalwart stewards, each of whom should have been carefully screened to make sure that he had no inclination toward either party. Lots were drawn as to which party should be to the right and which to the left. The right fell to the Magnets, the left to the Molybdenes. On the stage, and on the floor of the hall, and in every gallery, this division was observed. A wide aisle was left between the two parties, and throughout the meeting the neutral stewards marched up and down this aisle with stern orders to preserve the peace at all costs.

Aurora Bohra and Molly B. Dean had descended from their mountains to inspire their faithful followers on this momentous occasion. Each sat on a throne near the center of the stage, separated from the other only by the width of the aisle. Molly B. Dean loved all mankind, but she did not love Aurora Bohra; Aurora Bohra loved all mankind, but she did not love Molly B. Dean. Molly B. Dean, with sharp, black, snapping eyes, after surveying the gathering, darted a venomous glance upon Aurora Bohra, a glance so venomous that it must have shriveled a lesser personality. Aurora Bohra, after gazing raptly at the ceiling, allowed her great eyes to wander vaguely over the assembled multitude. Although at times her gaze seemed to be directed toward the opposite throne, it appeared that in that direction she saw nothing. The Medusa glances of Molly B. Dean passed her by. Only in the rapt contemplation of the great dome did she seem to yield to those sublime emotions which had made her what she was.

Mr. Tomkins and Mr. Merrow, each bristling with a sheaf of papers, stood at their desks, primed with all the facts and all the arguments most calculated to overwhelm the other party.

Immediately behind Zeruiah Tomkins sat his son and destined successor, Zachary. Zachary had been educated by his father with the most careful regard to the preservation of his orthodoxy. Never for a moment had he doubted the tenets of the Molybdenes, never for a moment had he imagined any other destiny than to help his father while he lived, and to carry on his work when death should call him to an even happier land. But, in spite of a diet adequately flavored with molybdenum, he was a somewhat weedy youth, and in his spare time turned his thoughts toward poetry rather than theology. Although molybdenum was supposed to confer muscular good cheer upon its devotees, he was the victim, to his secret shame, of a somewhat melancholy outlook. He thought Keat's *Ode to Autumn* unduly cheerful and wrote, himself, an *Ode to Autumn* beginning,

> Autumn leaves
> And barley sheaves
> Bring thought of the morrow
> And snow and sorrow.

Often he would take himself to task, and wish that he could achieve the eupeptic jollity which was the ideal of his sect. But, in spite of all his efforts, melancholy and languor invaded his inmost being whenever he could escape from the hustle and bustle of the Molybdene office.

Behind Manassah Merrow, and exactly opposite Zachary, sat Mr. Merrow's daughter, Leah. Leah, like Zachary, had been educated to the strictest orthodoxy. Like Zachary, it was intended that she should succeed her father. But, like Zachary, she had difficulty in preserving the state of mind demanded of an Adept. There were even dreadful moments when she could not bring herself to reverence Aurora. The time that she could spare from helping her father at the office, she spent at the piano. Mendelssohn was her favorite, but she rose occasionally to Chopin. Her real preference, however, was not for classical music, but for old-fashioned romantic songs such as *Gaily the Troubadour* and *The Bailiff's Daughter of Islington.*

She was not strictly beautiful, but her expression had a certain earnest exaltation and her eyes were large and sad.

Both Zachary and Leah, at the meeting, found themselves, as was natural, more interested in the opposite party than in their own. Zachary bestowed a brief glance upon Aurora Bohra, but shrank in revulsion from her vastness. Leah, encountering for a moment the piercing glance of Molly B. Dean, was so filled with terror that she longed to hide. Each, after this moment of alarm, was consoled by the sight of equal alarm across the aisle. Their eyes met. Each had supposed until that moment that all who supported the opposite faction were base and wicked. Each, meeting those frightened eyes, experienced a shock. "Surely," each thought, "it is nothing villainous that those eyes express! Can my dear father have been mistaken? Is it possible that the feelings which I experience may also exist in the breast of an opponent? Can it be that there is a common humanity which might override these differences?" And while each so thought, each continued to gaze into the eyes of the other.

Meanwhile, the business of the meeting proceeded, though the two young people were at first scarcely conscious of what was going on around them.

The Professor rose to deliver his opening address, which he had prepared with the utmost care, and of which he and the Prime Minister had conned every word to eliminate the slightest hint of criticism or lack of neutrality. Somewhat nervously he cleared his throat and began:

"Revered Pythonesses, Ladies and Gentlemen, we are all aware that in this great gathering there is disagreement ["Hear, Hear!" from all parts of the hall], but there is one matter as to which we are, I trust and believe, all at one. All of us are eager to seek truth, and when found to proclaim it."

From both sides of the hall a vast shout went up at these words, a shout of "No, No! Not on the other side!" The poor Professor, somewhat disconcerted, skipped several mellifluous phrases, and continued, "Well, be that as it may, it has been decided, by men for whose wisdom I have a profound respect, that the division of our great country into rival factions brings with it now, as it did in the days of the Wars of the Roses, as it did again in the lamentable dissensions of King and Parliament in the seventeenth century, a danger lest, absorbed in internal quarrels, we should lose sight of the peril from overseas. It is because of this peril that this meeting has been convened in the hope that, without any loss of fervor, without any diminution in the profundity of religious conviction, the two creeds may unite and forge, by their union, a weapon of irresistible might for the repelling of whatever enemies may threaten our national life."

At this point, again, he was interrupted. Cries came from everywhere: "That's easy! Let the others join *us!*" Again, the Professor skipped some pages of his prepared address, since he deemed it wise, in view of the temper of the meeting, to make an end quickly. "It is not for me," he concluded, "to dictate the agreement to be arrived at. This is for you to decide, since we live in a democracy. I will only repeat that the occasion is momentous, and that your responsibility is great. May God bless your deliberations!"

Even during these opening remarks it had become clear that the temper of the meeting was difficult. The unusual course was adopted of having the order of the proceedings announced not by the chairman, but by the Commissioner of Police. In authoritative tones, very unlike those of the Professor, he announced that each side would be allowed three speakers, each to speak for twenty minutes, and that the toss of a coin had allotted the first speech to the Molybdenes. He announced also that he had in reserve a large force of police, and that, at the first sign of disorder, the hall would be cleared. Somewhat cowed, the audience became for a time subdued, and listened to the first two speeches without excessive interruption.

These speeches were made by Mr. Tomkins and Mr. Merrow. Each dealt with the merits and success of his own movement, and studiously refrained from any mention of his rivals. There were coughs and yawns, and not a few, overcome by the oppressive atmosphere, fell asleep. It seemed as if the whole meeting would end in flat boredom. But there were fireworks in reserve. When Mr. Merrow sat down, Mr. Tomkins called upon Mr. Thorney to address the meeting. Mr. Thorney, from his very first words, showed no disposition to be conciliatory:

"Ladies and Gentlemen and Northern Magnets," he began. "I am the Head of the Molybdenic Secret Service. I know things that you do not know. I know the income of Sir Magnus North. I know the extent of his estates in the Northwest Territory. I know that every evening he spends many hours, whether in lascivious or merely lucrative commerce I know not, with the supposed Holy Woman, Miss Bohra."

By these words the meeting was, for a moment, completely stunned. The Magnets had known Mr. Thorney as a friend. The Molybdenes were finding difficulty in his new role. While the meeting was still held in bewildered silence, Mr. Wagner leaped up and shouted:

"You have listened to lies, but *I* will tell you truth! What do you know of Amalgamated Metals Inc.? What do you know of the fortune of its principal shareholder? What do you know of the role of molybdenum in its transactions? I, as Head of the Secret Service of the Magnets, I can give you the amazing answer: the fortune is immense; it is based upon molybdenum; and its lucky owner is the Widow Dean!"

By the time he sat down, both sides were wrought to the utmost pitch of fury. "Death to Sir Magnus and shame on his infamous paramour!" was shouted from one side. "Down with grasping plutocrats! To the gallows with Murderous Molly!" the other side retorted. For a brief moment their co-operative efforts were devoted to overcoming a posse of stewards. That done, the rival Saints met in savage mêlée. The police, who had retained their coherence, cleared the hall with tear gas. With streaming eyes and thunderous sneezes, the disconcerted thousands poured into the street. Revived by the outer air, they resumed the fray in disorganized groups. Clothes were torn from backs, blows were exchanged, feet were stamped upon, objurgations were shouted. Late into the night the vague tumult continued, until at last, utterly exhausted, the Holy Combatants fell asleep upon the cold pavement.

CHAPTER VII

The leading personages on the stage, meanwhile, had been exhorted by the police to make use of a secret exit. The chairman, feeling that his functions could no longer be exercised, was very willing to depart. The Nepalese delegate, who had felt disaster coming, tapped the Professor on the shoulder and said, "Let me take care of you." The two together were hustled into a police car. "Oh, where shall we go?" said the Professor. "To the Nepalese Embassy," said his new friend. Arriving there tired and hopeless, he was slowly revived by kindness, and when he had had time to collect his thoughts, he was offered a professorship in his own subject in the Himalayan University of Nepal, provided he would sign a document in a language unknown to him. He did so, and, having thus established his credentials, which, as he discovered long afterward, consisted of a statement to the effect that Tensing had been the first to reach the summit of Everest, he was taken by plane to the seat of his new academic activities. At the end of ten years he produced his monumental work, *Religion and Superstition among the Aborigines of the West*. But this work has not appeared in any European language.

The two priestesses presented the police with a difficult problem. Oblivious of everything else, Molly B. Dean had rushed across the aisle to make a frenzied assault upon the massive Aurora. Reaching up with her nails, she made long bloody scratches upon the face of her rival, who, with her open hand, gave her a push, which knocked her flat upon the floor. "Harridan!" she shouted as she lay prone. "Peculating virago!" Aurora retorted in a voice very different from, and much more shrill than, that to which her disciples were accustomed. Some policemen picked up Molly B. Dean, while ten others, with drawn truncheons, propelled Aurora Bohra. Both together were placed in a Black Maria, where, across an intervening wall of policemen, they continued to hurl insults at each other. Both were accused of a breach of the peace, and they were confined for the night in separate cells which invited far from pleasant reflections.

Mr. Tomkins and Mr. Merrow, neither of whom had expected the intemperate intervention of their secret agents, retired under police protection to their respective offices. There, deeply dejected, with their heads buried in their hands, they contemplated the ruin of their lifework. Although total abstinence, except in the Recreative Palaces, was a rigid tenet of both sects, both these devoted men were found by charwomen in the morning prone on the floor with an empty bottle beside each.

As for Zachary and Leah, they had been so absorbed in each other that they were not aware of what was going on about them until the din became overwhelming. Sitting among the neutrals, a little way behind them, was Ananias Wagthorne, an official of the Ministry of Culture, who had been sent to obtain data for any bureaucratic action that might be called for. He was a kindly and perceptive person, and had observed their absorption in each other. In the final confusion he extended a hand to each, and said, "Let me escort you to safety." Although somewhat embarrassed by each other's presence, they obeyed, since any other course seemed difficult. Helped by the police, he extricated them and conveyed them safely to his flat. He introduced them to his wife, who listened understandingly to his account of the monumental fiasco. His wife was a good-natured lady, filled with sympathy for the young people. "I do not think," she said to her husband, "that these young people ought to attempt to go to their homes tonight. The streets are disturbed, and no one can tell what furious mobs may do. If Mr. Zachary could be content with the drawing-room sofa, Miss Leah could have the spare room, and both could stay here for the night." Both accepted gratefully. And both, utterly worn out, soon fell asleep.

As the great meeting had been held on a Saturday, Mr. Wagthorne was able to stay at home next morning, and devoted himself to comforting the young people and diminishing their perplexities. Neither knew what to believe of the lurid revelations to which they had listened. Could it be that the Molybdenic faith was built upon financial fraud? Zachary's thoughts shuddered away from so dreadful a possibility. Could it be that the faith of the Magnets was only an incident in the rise of Sir Magnus North to wealth and power? This nightmare suggestion seemed to Leah to empty life of all its purpose. Mr. Wagthorne, finding them disconsolate, and with no appetite for their breakfasts, inquired into their doubts. "Can these things be true?" they both asked him.

"I fear they are but too true," he replied. "It has been my official duty to make inquiries as to both sects. From the Board of Trade, I have ascertained the extent of Mrs. Dean's interests in Amalgamated Metals Inc.; and from the Administration of the Northwest Territory, I have discovered the vast area possessed by Sir Magnus, and its almost unlimited possibility of mineral wealth. The relation of Sir Magnus with Aurora Bohra has long been known and watched by the police. Your fathers, my dear young people, were, I am convinced, totally ignorant of the revelations that were made at yesterday's meeting. They, I am sure, are honestly and wholeheartedly persuaded that the doctrines they preach are both true and beneficent. It may be that, when you have had time to reflect, each of you will agree with his or her father, and continue to believe as heretofore. But I think it more likely that you will both perceive what I believe to be the facts in this painful situation, and that you will learn to build your lives upon a firmer foundation than that upon which they have rested hitherto.

"But is it possible," both exclaimed, "that any movement

so vast, and so potent in moving men's minds, should be based upon nothing but fraud and folly?"

"It is only too possible," he replied. "It has been my duty to study the history of such movements. They have been numerous. Some have flourished briefly, others have lasted for centuries. But there is no relation whatever between the vitality and life of a movement and its basis in good sense."

At this point he fetched from his shelves a large tome called *The Dictionary of Sects, Heresies, Ecclesiastical Parties, and Schools of Religious Thought.*

"Do not imagine," he said, "that you have any reason for shame, or that you differ from the rest of mankind in the capacity to believe what afterward appears to have been nonsense. In this volume the similar follies of the last two thousand years are recorded, and a little study will show you that, in comparison with many of these, your creeds have been sensible and moderate. Both your heresies begin with the letter M, so let us see what this book has to say under this letter. Let me recommend you to study the doctrines of Macarius. I can assure you they are well deserving of attention, as are those of the Majorinians, and the Malakanes, and the Marcellinians, and the Marcosians, and the Masbothians, and the Melchisedechians, and the Metangismonitae, and the Morelstschiki, and the Muggletonians. Take, for example, the Marcosians, who followed Marcus the Magician, 'a perfect adept in magical impostures . . . joining the buffooneries of Anaxilaus to the craftiness of the Magi,' and by these arts seducing the wives of deacons, and justifying unlimited license by the doctrine that he had 'attained to a height above all power,' and was therefore free to act in every respect as he pleased. Or, again, you may be thankful that neither of you belong to the sect of the Morelstschiki, whose 'custom is to meet together on a certain day in the year in some retired place, and having dug a deep pit, to fill it with wood, straw, and other combustibles, while they are singing weird hymns relating to the ceremony. Fire is then applied to the piled-up fuel, and numbers leap into the midst of it, stimulated by the triumphant hymns of those around, to purchase a supposed martyrdom by their suicidal act.' No, my dear young friends, you need not feel that you have been exceptional in folly, for folly is natural to man. We consider ourselves distinguished from the ape by the power of thought. We do not remember that it is like the power of walking in a one-year-old. We think, it is true, but we think so badly that I often feel it would be better if we did not. But I have matters that I must attend to, and, for the moment, I will leave you to each other."

Left *tête-à-tête* they preserved at first an embarrassed silence. Then Zachary said, hesitatingly, "I cannot yet disentangle what I am to think of what we heard yesterday, and of what our kind friend has been saying. But there is one thing of which I feel sure, and which I will say: When I looked across the aisle and saw the crystal purity and gentle charity that shone from your eyes, I could no longer believe that all Northern Magnets are degraded beings."

"Oh, Mr. Tomkins," she replied, "I am glad you have said what you did, and . . . and . . . I . . . felt the same about the Molybdenes."

"Oh, Miss Merrow," he replied, "can it be that, amid such ruin, something has been salvaged? Drifting alone, parted by doubt and despair from former companions and former hopes, may I think that in this night of apparent solitude we have found each other?"

"I think you may, Mr. Tomkins," she said.

And with that they fell into each other's arms.

For a little while they forgot their sorrows in mutual ecstasy; but presently Leah sighed, and said: "But, Zachary, what are we to *do*? Can we break our fathers' hearts? But how can we do otherwise? It is impossible that we should marry and should continue to profess our several former tenets."

"No," he replied, "that would be impossible. We must tell our fathers of our loss of faith, whatever may be the pain to them. You and I henceforth, dear Leah, must be one in thought and word and deed, and that will be impossible if we pretend to a divided allegiance."

With heavy hearts, they decided to confront their fathers. But, strengthened by the new fire of love, neither faltered before the ordeal.

CHAPTER VIII

Zachary and Leah, after some further conversation, decided to postpone to the next day their confrontation with their respected fathers, the rather as the Wagthornes had very kindly asked them to stay another night. After luncheon they walked in Kensington Gardens, and, having known until that time nothing but offices throughout the week and big meeting halls on Sundays, they were struck by the beauty of wild nature and enjoyed emotions for which others have to travel to the Alps or the Victoria Falls.

"I begin to think," said Zachary, as he feasted his eyes upon a multicolored bed of tulips, "that perhaps we have lived, hitherto, with somewhat too limited preoccupations.

These tulips, I am convinced, owe nothing to molybdenum."

"How refreshing are your words of wisdom!" Leah replied. "Magnetism also, I am persuaded, has done nothing to produce this wild loveliness."

They agreed that they felt themselves expanding in mind and heart with every moment that passed since they had escaped from the bondage of dogma. They had been brought up to worship brawn, in which neither excelled. They had been taught to despise everything delicate and subtle, everything fragile and evanescent. Zachary, with secret shame, had enjoyed anthologies of the poets, but he had felt about this as a secret morphia addict might feel about his surreptitious doses. She, in her stolen hours at the piano, had preferred the times when she knew her father to be absent. But fortunately he had no ear for music, and, on the occasions when he discovered her at the instrument, she persuaded him that she was studying the Magnetic hymnbook. Now at last they felt that they need no longer be ashamed of their tastes.

But they were still not without their fears—fears for the world as well as for themselves. "Do you think," she asked him with some hesitation, "that it is possible to be good without the help of faith? I have lived, hitherto, a blameless life. I have never uttered a bad word. I have never tasted alcohol. I have never suffered the pulmonary pollution of tobacco. Never have I slept with my head pointing elsewhere than to the Magnetic Pole. Never have I gone to bed too late or risen after the prescribed hour. And I have found this same devotion to duty among my friends. But will it be possible to go on living so, when I no longer feel that my every action and my every breath should be a service of devotion and homage to Earth, the Great Magnet?"

"Alas," he replied, "the same perplexities trouble me. I fear that I may be content in the morning to touch my toes fewer than ninety-nine times, and even perhaps to acquiesce in a lukewarm bath. I can no longer feel quite certain that alcohol and tobacco lead to Hell. What, with such doubts, is to become of us? Shall we go down the primrose path to moral degradation and physical ruin? What is to preserve us, what is to preserve others who have hitherto been our co-religionists, from a gradual descent into drunkenness, debauchery and disaster? What, when we meet our fathers, shall we say when they argue, as argue they will, that creeds such as theirs, whether true or false, are necessary for the preservation of mankind? I do not yet see the way to a clear answer. But let us hope that parental wrath will inspire us when the moment comes."

"I hope it may be so," she said, "but I confess that I have fears, for, even while strengthened by dogma, neither of us was wholly able to abstain from sin. You with your poets, and I with my piano, were guilty of deceit. If even in the past we sinned, what will become of us now?"

Oppressed by this solemn thought, they returned gravely and silently to the Wagthornes' tea table.

When Monday morning came they sought their respective fathers, determined to make such explanations as should be necessary, and to seek such conciliation as might be possible. Zachary found his father at the office surrounded by a wild confusion. Letters of resignation were piled high upon his desk. Scathing articles in hitherto friendly newspapers were omens of ruin. After a Sunday devoted to recuperation, most of those who had fought each other as devotees of this sect or that had come to the conclusion that both equally must be repudiated. On Saturday night, half the mob had sided with Mr. Tomkins, and half with Mr. Merrow. Now, though it was not the time of day for a mob, the few who passed either office showed equal hostility to both, and only a strong force of police protected the faithful remnant from the united hostility of those who felt that they had been duped. Mr. Tomkins, though he retained his faith, was unable to understand the designs of Providence in permitting what had occurred. When he saw Zachary, a gleam of returning hope appeared for a moment upon his countenance.

"Ah, my dear son," he said, "to what tribulations are the good exposed. But you—you whom, from your earliest infancy, I have educated in the True Faith, you whose blameless life and unfaltering belief have been among the greatest joys of my arduous existence, you, I am sure, will not desert me in this difficult hour. I am no longer young, and to build up again from its first foundations that great Church, which had come so near to final triumph, may prove beyond the power of my declining years. But you, with the fresh vigor of youth, with the impetuous ardor of one who has never had to fight doubt or uncertainty, you, I feel, will rebuild the ruined edifice more pure, more splendid, more shining than that which Saturday's fell work has laid in ruins."

Zachary was deeply moved, and his eyes filled with tears. He wished with all his heart that he could give the answer which his father longed to hear. But he could not. Something even more compelling than intellectual doubts as to the physiological benefits of molybdenum prevented his acquiescence. The thought of Leah made submission to his father impossible. Never could his father consent, with any willingness, to union with a Northern Magnet. Zachary realized that he must speak, no matter how great might be his father's pain.

"Father," he said, "much as I feel for your sorrow, I cannot do as you wish. I have lost my faith. Molybdenum, we are assured, cures diseases of the chest, but you must have known, or at least suspected, that I suffer from tuberculosis of the lung. We are told that molybdenum makes our muscles strong, but every godless hooligan from the slums can defeat me in a wrestling match. For these things, however, some explanation could perhaps be found. What is more difficult is that I love Leah Merrow. . . ."

"Leah Merrow!" gasped his father.

"Yes, Leah Merrow, and she has consented to become my wife. She, like me, can no longer believe the faith in which she has been brought up. She, like me, is determined to accept painful facts, however they may shatter a cherished world of beliefs. It is not your work, it is not the work of Mr. Merrow, that can inspire our lives henceforth. We wish to live unfettered by dogma, free to accept whatever the facts may indicate, with minds open to the winds of heaven, not wrapped in the cotton wool of some warm and comfortable system!"

"Oh, Zachary," his father answered, "you wring my heart! You turn the bayonet in the dreadful wound! Is it not enough that the world has turned against me? Must my own son join my enemies? Oh, dreadful day! And it is not I alone, it is the whole world that you will be bringing to ruin by your heartless levity. What do you know of human nature? How can you estimate the wild anarchic forces that your 'free winds of heaven' will liberate? What do you imagine restrains men from murder, arson, pillage and debauchery? Do you imagine that the puny forces of reason can effect this great work? Alas, in your sheltered life, you have been kept from knowledge of the darker side of human nature. You have believed that gentleness and goodness grow naturally in the human heart. You have not realized that they are the unnatural outgrowth of unnatural beliefs. It is such beliefs that I have tried to inculcate. And, in this dark hour, I can admit that the Northern Magnets also have been engaged in this task. Our creed, I still believe, was as superior to theirs as the noonday sun to the last glimmer of twilight. But what *you* offer is not twilight, it is black, impenetrable night. And, in the night, what deeds of darkness may be done! If this is to be your work, there will have to be, between you and me, an enmity more deep and more implacable than that which had divided me from the Northern Magnets."

Contrary to his own expectations, Zachary reacted to this speech in a manner quite different from that intended by his father. "No!" he said. "No! It is not by organized falsehood that mankind is to be saved. While you imagined that you were building virtue, what was it that you were really building? It was the fortune of Molly B. Dean. You imagined her a Holy Woman. Was it holiness that inspired her when she scratched the face of Aurora Bohra? Was it holiness that made her hide her financial interest in the anonymity of Amalgamated Metals Inc.? And, to come nearer home, do you realize that you were sacrificing my life to your credulity? Do you realize that you have refused me the treatment that my body demands, because it was not that that your sect prescribes? Can you not see that here, in my own case, is a sample of the evils that men must suffer when they substitute dogma for fact? I will not believe that human nature is as bad as you say it is. But if indeed you are right in this, no system of imposed discipline will cure the evils, for those who impose the discipline will be inspired by their own evil passions, and will find some indirect way of inflicting the torments that their wickedness makes them desire. No, you will but systematize evil; and evil, reduced to a system, is more dreadful than anything that untamed anarchic passion can produce. Goodby, Father! My love and my sympathy are yours, but not, henceforth, my work!"

With these words, he departed.

Leah's interview with her father pursued a similar course, and came to a similar termination. Mr. Tomkins and Mr. Merrow each attempted to continue the old work, but the fickle wind of fashion had deserted them and only a few, and those in out-of-the-way suburbs, remained faithful. Mr. Tomkins and Mr. Merrow were compelled to vacate their palatial offices for which Mrs. Dean and Sir Magnus no longer thought it worth while to pay. Both men, having become dependent upon the voluntary offerings of the faithful remnant, sank into poverty.

Sir Magnus and Molly B. Dean, though both suffered considerable losses, remained rich, and largely recouped themselves by pooling their interests. In consequence of this, the friction between the United States and Canada ceased, and governments smiled upon their joint enterprise. Aurora Bohra, who could not believe that her success had depended upon Sir Magnus's money, remained at the sanatorium and welcomed as before the few guests who still came. But gradually the place became derelict, and the few faithful observed a decay in her powers. The more fanatical among the remaining Adherents attributed her decline to the malignant influence of molybdenum, and darkly suspected her of apostasy; but, alas, the evidence for a simpler explanation became gradually overwhelming. She sank first into alcoholic excesses, and then still deeper into the baleful dominion of hashish. At length it became necessary to carry her off, raving and maniacal, and leave her to end her days in a mental home.

Zachary and Leah, who had never known want, and had taken it for granted that they would follow their fathers in their comfortable and well-paid positions, found themselves in urgent need of some means of livelihood. Zachary, who had impressed Mr. Wagthorne by his capacity for absorbing an entirely new point of view, and who had, in his surreptitious reading, acquired a considerable breadth of knowledge, was found, on Mr. Wagthorne's recommendation, worthy of a minor post in the Ministry of Culture. Helped by Mrs. Wagthorne to establish themselves in a tiny flat, Zachary and Leah married.

Leah, absorbed in domestic cares and in her love for Zachary, found no time to repine, and did not hanker after former certainties. But Zachary found adjustment more difficult. Formerly, decisions had been easy; now, they were hard. Should he do this or do that? Should he believe this or believe that? He found himself beset by hesitations and without a compass by which to steer his course. He acquired the habit of spending his Sundays in long, solitary walks.

One winter evening, returning weary through drizzle and fog, he found himself outside a tin tabernacle where a remnant of the Molybdenes still worshiped. To the accompaniment of the harmonium, they were singing those well-known words:

> Molybdenum of metals best
> Is good for high and low.
> It cures diseases of the chest
> And makes our muscles grow.

He sighed, and muttered to himself, "Could I but return to the old sublimities! Ah, how hard is the Life of Reason!"

ABOUT THE AUTHOR

BERTRAND ARTHUR WILLIAM RUSSELL *received the Nobel Prize for literature in 1950. He is the grandson of Lord John Russell, the British Foreign Secretary during the Civil War. Before going to Cambridge he was educated at home by governesses and tutors, acquiring a thorough knowledge of German and French; and it has been said that his "admirable and lucid English style may be attributed to the fact that he did not undergo a classical education at a public school." Certainly, this style is perceptible in the many books that have flowed from his pen during half a century—books that have shown him to be the most profound of mathematicians, the most brilliant of philosophers, and the most lucid of popularizers. His most recent major works are* A History of Western Philosophy, *published in 1945;* Human Knowledge: Its Scope and Limits, *published in 1948;* Authority and the Individual, *published in 1949;* Unpopular Essays, *that grossly mistitled book, published in 1951;* New Hopes for a Changing World, *published in 1952;* The Impact of Science on Society, *published in 1953;* Satan in the Suburbs, *published in 1953; and* Human Society in Ethics and Politics, *published in 1955.*